AUTHOR'S NOTE

I dedicate my book to all women and men and to those who want to know more about a job which has been too much glamorized and which is often presented in a very fictitious way. After working 5 years as call girl in London I decided to write and share the truth about this job which is often misunderstood and misjudged by both men and women. The names I used in my book are the figment of my imagination, but the stories are true and the facts are depicted in the way I perceived and felt at the moment of their occurrence. I must thank all my former clients who inspired me to write the book and who I hope will make an effort to read it. As a non native English speaker I hope that I portrayed my experiences in a way that could be easily understood and hope from the bottom of my heart that my readers will not be disappointed. I have chosen to write under the name of Julia Cooper which is an alias.

AF373985

Most inner thoughts...

Who are you? I said to myself while I was staring at my own image in the bathroom mirror. All of a sudden I felt old and tired , too tired to care about anything.   I wanted to escape reality as I have done in the past when an expensive shopping spree would have cheered me up instantly. I looked at the numerous perfume bottles laid on the marble table with no interest,   I had no desire for an expensive shopping spree; my appetite was jaded. I felt like there was something missing in my life, I wanted to leave the past behind. I wanted to do something different and meaningful. How could I let myself go astray and choose to sell my body for money? I wanted to start to write again as I did so many years ago when I have been working as a journalist. I wanted to share my most intimate thoughts and my experiences with all women. I wanted them to know the truth in simple words, about a job which has been perhaps too much glamorized.

Call girl escort, prostitute or whore for more than 5 years, yes that was my glamorous job in London and sadly a path to unhappiness and loneliness. But I have come to understand myself and men better and hope that women will understand themselves and men better after they would have read my book. I have always wondered what made men come to me and pay for sex or companionship as I have never seen myself as a beauty. I can certainly tell you that married or single, most men will always be attracted by such women, hoping to experience something different or something unusual. I could not help notice that most of my clients were married men. I was often overwhelmed with guilt and remorse. I started to think of the woman they had at home. Was she young? Was she pretty? Did she know? Was he nice to her? Despite all my misgivings concerning my job I knew that it was better for me to be on the other side as I'm prone to sudden fits of jealousy. I could not conceive the idea of a man cheating on me. After 5 years during which I have seen and done almost everything I'm convinced that few men could truly be physically loyal to a woman and mostly those who have strongly religious beliefs.

Men cheat mentally probably at every 10 min; yes it is true, believe it or not. And with tones of porn available on internet every intention to stay loyal seems doomed. The easily accessible pornography has brought me more clients than I could physically and mentally handle. I'm talking about the men who had acquired toxic ideas about sex, marriage and relationships after watching pornography. Some of my client's taste for filthy and deviant fantasies could hardly be depicted into words. It was a job with a dark and damaging side and not at all glamorous.

How well do you know your partner and yourself? I have no intention to cast any doubts into your mind, I just want to offer you an incentive for introspection .How fulfilled are you sexually and how important is that to you? Do you think that a man could be loyal in a relationship and never cheat? Why men go to hookers? Is a married man really cheating when he pays for sex? How open-minded are you in terms of fulfilling his unusual or deviant fantasies?   I often thought of myself as being on the other side, the cheated wife or the cheated girlfriend. I struggled trying to understand why men cannot get enough with one woman and wondered if they felt any remorse after our encounter.

 Why would a man pay for sex? And why would he do that with a woman who is often less attractive than you? Single or in a relationship, married or unmarried men go to escorts for different reasons. Some men would simply come to see me because they could not cope with loneliness. My sweetest encounters had been with the single elderly men who genuinely told me that they craved companionship and a warm body.

    "My wife died long time go .I missed being touched."

    "My wife and I got divorced many years ago. I did not want to marry again and go through the same thing.

    They caressed my body and kissed me with almost a painful adulation and made me shed many tears after they would have left. I knew what loneliness was, I knew how painful it must have been. It was undoubtedly the most rewarding feeling , I was the doer of a good deed .I have been giving tenderness and pleasure and joy to men who have been deprived of it. There is certainly a big difference between young men and old men in terms of fantasizing and making love to a woman. The older men were more romantic and very fond of long foreplay.

    "I want to make you come," they whispered into my ear as they seemed to care less about their own pleasure.

They were so far the most enjoyable encounters as they somehow made me forget about my own unhappiness. As men get older they become a more refined version of the older self and I can tell you that they definitely knew how to push the right button.

 The young men would visit me for different reasons, it was either boredom or they just wanted to experience something new, and often wanted to put into practice some of the stuff they must have seen in the porn movies. I was shocked with the deviant nature of their fantasies and realized how much harm the porn addiction had done to them. Some were young boys addicted to pornography who probably were masturbating three times a day and could not get an erection in my presence. It made me angry as I could not make them come.

"I do not understand why you come here, "I shouted, trying to maintain my composure as I did not want to lose a client.

My mouth was sucking his cock fast trying to make him reach the climax. My cheeks hurt so badly after sucking his cock for 45 minutes. I told him politely that we had to stop.

"You can rest for 10 minutes. I can pay for another half an hour," he said in a very relaxed voice.

I was terrified, I knew that I could not go longer than one hour. My cheeks and my tongue were numb with so much sucking.

"You have to come sweetheart or accept that you might be leaving without coming. I can't go longer than one hour .I cannot feel my tongue and my lips and my cheeks hurt."

"I will come, no worries. Give me the phone."

I did what I was told with the utmost speed.

"Keep rubbing and sucking, I will come."

I could hear a woman and a man moaning, followed by dirty talking and loud slapping noises. His body quivered and semen came out in fitful spasms .His phone fell from his hand. I was exhausted, shocked and somewhat disgusted, seeing a handsome young boy who could not come without watching porn. I was there fully naked and giving him best blow job and yet, it was not enough. I felt so bad that I almost wanted to tell him that I will not be seeing him again.

" You are such a handsome young boy. You should find a girlfriend. "

"Yeah, like that would be so easy, "he said, closing the door behind him.

I was overwhelmed with sadness as I sensed some kind of pessimistic resignation in the tone of his remark. I could not understand why all these handsome young men would pay for sex with a woman who was 40 years old. They could have had a young, sweet girl .I wondered if they could relate to her in a satisfactory way in real life as their minds had been very much poisoned by the constant watching of pornography .The habit of masturbating daily was far the most damaging as it would have weaken their bodies and would have made them impotent before they reached their 40s.

The girlfriend experience, yes, I almost forgot about it .To my surprise, occasionally some of the young men would ask about girlfriend experience and French kissing. I was more than happy to accept it as they reminded me of my giddy youth, how much I desired to be again in my 20s. Their young bodies and their soft skin combined with a certain amount of innocence made me feel young again. They were young boys whose minds have not been poisoned by constant watching of pornography. They felt lonely and just wanted a good time with a woman, which in real life would have been more difficult to achieve.

"Don't you have a girlfriend?" I asked them almost every time, curious to find out why they would pay for sex with me.

"I cannot afford it now, it is much cheaper for me this way. "

I knew that in London everything was expensive, but not this. I could not understand it.

"It would cost me double to take her out, go to restaurant or buy her presents."

It was the most common answer to my question. I could not regret any of these encounters as I always had the best sex with young men .They had incredible stamina and were able to have erection more than once. I always ended up exhausted and begun to worry about my next client; I hated to fake orgasms. However, emotionally the most rewarding experiences have been with the elderly gentlemen as they were more mature in regards to conversation and very fond of long foreplay. It was the quality that made the experience so valuable, and not the quantity.

The domination stuff was quite popular among both young and older men and money was in the beginning the only incentive for offering such services. I found them degrading. I grew up in a Christian community and could not understand how could somebody go so low? I could not get rid of that image in the end of the day when I climbed up to my bed. Pet treatment, having them walk like dogs and flogging them with my crop, spitting on their faces and asking them to lick my boots.

"It is all about acting .You just have to play the part well and make it look as genuine as possible," I thought to myself, smiling.

 The cock torture was the thing that was beyond my comprehension. Why would a lovely young man want that? I would have naturally expected him to be outside sitting on a bench with a lovely girl. I could not find any explanation besides the assumption that they must have gone through some kind of trauma in their childhood. In a strange way I was expecting older men to be more interested in cock torture and domination, in latex and rough stuff.

Most of the young men wanted to do something unusual and in some cases to try something very deviant and filthy, all fuelled undoubtedly by the amount of porn they watched daily.

"Do you do fisting?"

"Are you into anal and double penetration?"

"Can I bring a friend?"

"Do you do mouth fucking or face abuse?"

"Do you swallow?"

"Do you do orgies? Can I bring some friends?"

"Do you do sloppy and deep throat?"

These were the kind of questions I resented most. I loathed abnormal, deviant sexual behaviour as I found it degrading. It was unacceptable to simply objectify women, to see them as a hole for a cock and mercilessly thrust into it until a woman chokes .I wondered if men and women were doing this a thousand years ago. I'm sure that men and women discovered the joy of pleasing each other orally, but not to this extent when it becomes an aberration.

The minds of young and old men have been poisoned by the abundance and accessibility of pornography and who could be the best person to fulfil their fantasies if not the escort girls. It is enough one click and men can satisfy their darkest and filthiest desires, indulging a fantasy that they could never try with somebody in a normal relationship.

The 30 min stepmother abuse...

The most funniest and unusual fantasy was the stepmother role-play. It was a student who wanted me to play being his stepmother, who would take advantage of him in his sleep, taking his clothes off and abusing him sexually. I always found role play very demanding as you had to participate in and make it as real as possible. Our meetings were brief, but very intense. It started from the moment he entered the door and followed our previously discussed scenario step by step.

"Oh mommy I missed you, "he said to me, kissing my cheeks and hugging me.

I did not have children of my own and never been a stepmother so seeing a grown up addressing to me that way made me feel awkward .I bit my upper lip as hard as I could , not wanting to burst into a laughter and ruin all our role play session. I was paid to fulfil his fantasy and I did not want to hurt his feelings.

"I'm going to bed mommy, "he said, starting to undress and keeping only his underwear.

" Mommy will look after you, do not worry, "I said, caressing his cheeks with my finger and kissing his forehead.

My thoughts went astray as I tucked him in and wondered what would have been like to have children of my own. Lying on the bed with his eyes closed he looked so young and vulnerable. I looked at him and smiled. I knew that in real life I could have never been able to do this and I was fully aware that it was no harm it; it was just a fantasy. The tip of my fingers lingered on his lovely full lips.I kissed him and lifted the cover slowly , touching his penis through his underwear. It was limp as he controlled himself very well pretending to be deep asleep.

"That is not going to last long, "I thought to myself smiling.

 I removed his underwear slowly and I kissed and caressed his balls and cock with my tongue, watching it turn into an almost monster size cock. I have never been fond of a big size as I could not put up with the pain of being stretched in order to accommodate a big penis. I grabbed a condom and rolled it down to the base of his penis along with a good amount of lube. I positioned the monster near the entrance of my vagina and pushed against it. I could feel its huge head stretching my vagina as it went deeper and deeper, and despite the considerable amount of lube applied I felt stretched beyond bearable. All of a sudden he opened his eyes and started to wriggle his hips, his hands flailing as if he wanted to stop me.

"Mommy, oh mommy what are you doing? Does daddy know? "he asked pretending to be shocked.

"Keep quiet, "I replied, pressing the palm of my hand against his lips, hoping to muffle whatever sounds might have come out of his mouth. We have been doing this for many times and I knew that he liked it a little rough, but we never crossed our boundaries.

" Daddy is too old. Mommy needs young cock, "I replied, riding him wildly while my hips were almost crushing his legs.

" Mommy stop, stop it! What are you doing? If daddy finds out?" he whispered, trying to remove my hand from his mouth and wriggling his hips as if he wanted to free himself from the weight of my body.

"He won't if you keep your mouth shut, "I said, pressing my hand harder. I started to ride him faster and faster.

"Give it to mommy, do it now! "I shouted, freeing his mouth from the pressure of my hand and faking a big orgasm.

"I'm coming mommy, I'm coming! "he whispered hoarsely, pushing his hips frantically and pounding into me mercilessly. Beads of sweat were running from his forehead over his cheeks as he laid there utterly exhausted.

"That must have been something, "I said with a crooked smile.

"Yeah, I have to focus hard on my fantasy if I want to come. I can come only with you this way. I have been only once with another escort before, but she was not good. I could not come and maybe because I could not connect with her."

"I'm happy to hear that and hope to see you again soon," I responded, giving him a big hug.

" You should be a sex teacher. I'm going to send my wife to you to groom her when I get married," he said , walking towards the door.

He remained one of my very regular clients probably for the simple reason that he could not feel comfortable enough to fulfil his fantasy with any other escort girl. My ability to more or less empathize with my clients made me quite popular.

Sex lessons for a virgin...

"Do you offer sex lessons?"

"Sex lessons? What do you mean?" I answered puzzled. It was not the kind of question you would expect to hear when you work as an escort girl.

" Yes, I'm a virgin and I shall have my wedding soon. I want you to teach me everything about a woman. I want to learn how to give pleasure to my future wife."

"I think that can be arranged. But it might take more than an hour .Just let me know what day and what time is good for you. I would rather like you to be my first client as I want to do my best." He came to see me next day early in the morning and we had a fantastic time.

" I want you to take all your clothes off and lie on the bed. I want to look at your body and imagine my future wife. I want it to be like it was her instead of you." He touched my breasts softly and started to rub my nipples between his fingers.

"Kiss them and use your tongue gently. Remember to always do it gently as they are very sensitive." I felt my body warming up to an almost unbearable heat, his tongue was wet and hot and to my surprise he was very good at doing it. I knew he was going to be a very good lover to his wife.

"Do you like it?" He asked while his fingers were moving down to my navel.

"I do like it and you are very good at it. Play with your tongue there, most women love that too."

He circled my navel with the tip of his tongue and then moved it in and out so beautifully that It made me all wet down there .He stopped and looked at the narrow strip of hair , his index finger moved along it .

" I want to see it and explore it. I have never seen one in real life."

My mind could not conceive that. I could have never imagined that t virgin men could exist nowadays, except maybe for hermits. I opened my legs wide, allowing him to have a full view of my sex.

" You have a beautiful pussy, it looks like a pink rose."

" Spread the outer puffy lips gently and look at the small orifice. You can put your tongue there and play or you can insert your finger, but this has to be done gently."

"Do all of them look the same way?" he asked his finger moving so slowly along the outer puffy lips.

"They look more or less the same, but every woman is different and so is the size and the shape of her vulva." I took his hand in mine and moved his index just above the puffy outer lips.

" This is the magic button and almost any woman will come if you rub it lightly with your finger or if you flick it with the tip of your tongue." He started to circle my clit with his tongue, making me wriggle and moan loudly. I urged him to slide one finger inside my vagina.

" You will drive a woman insane and give her multiple orgasms if your tongue is flicking her clit while you move your finger inside there as fast as you can, "I whispered, trying to catch my breath as I was on the brink of experiencing the sweet death. Yes, I called it sweet death as it is an orgasm so powerful that you almost faint and you would be lying down motionless and speechless and overwhelmed with its sweet torpor.

" Are you ok?" He asked, puzzled to see that all of a sudden my hips stopped moving and could not say one single word.

" I need five minutes, "I said, closing my eyes and struggling to come out of my trance. Aware that our almost two hours had passed , he searched for his clothes and started to dress , casting a glance at me now and then to see if I regained my powers.

" Not all women will react the same way, but they will definitely have the most powerful orgasms when their clit and their G spot is stimulated that way. You pleased me beyond expectation and you are going to be a great lover to your wife."

"Thank You for your patience, I really want to please my wife and have a happy marriage. That's why I came to you. This was my first and my last encounter with an escort girl."

I was dying to have one question answered to as I did not want to ask him earlier and make him feel embarrassed.

"Why did you choose to remain a virgin? This sounds so unusual, I mean coming from a man."

"It was not for religious reasons, I wanted to keep myself pure for my wife. I did not want our love to be tainted by my sexual experiences with other women. I wanted us both to discover it together for the first time."

I deeply wished the best to both, hoping that he will keep his promise for the rest of his life. I knew that there was no certainty of a long lasting relationship especially now with so many temptations when with a simple click a man can buy sex and pleasure anytime, even in the comfort of his own home, while his spouse or girlfriend might be doing the dishes .I have always wondered who is more likely to cheat, the man or the woman? Since I have not seen too many men advertising for gigolo jobs I'm more inclined to think that escorting jobs for women are in higher demand and consequently men are more likely to cheat.

Some of the very young men who came to see me were drug addicts or even drug dealers. They always wanted to sniff a line or two when they arrived or before they left and kindly asked me if I wanted any. I have always stayed away from drugs or any substance that would cause addiction, except for my early caffeine fix. I could not allow it to interfere with my business or to put my safety at risk, so I avoided any substance which could have impaired my ability to reason. Besides that I hated the idea of addiction in any of its forms as I strongly believed that you could not be truly free that way.

Meeting a gangster...

My phone rang unusually early that day. I wondered who could be as I usually started in the afternoon.

"Do you meet gangsters?"

"It depends, I have always liked Bugsy Malone, "I replied, bursting into laughter.

"I'm Bugsy Malone .Can I see you at 10 this morning?"

" That can be arranged, though I do not take bookings so early .But I will make an exception for you, "I answered, wondering what was behind all that.

He must have been drunk or maybe he was under the influence of some drug and was hallucinating .I began to worry slightly and not wanting to ruin maybe the most exciting experience I rushed to my wardrobe and took out a black long dress covered with spangles. I put it on and stared at my body in the mirror for good minutes. It was so flattering to my body, not too tight and not too large and all I needed to make it perfect was some nice make up. I applied a thin layer of deep red lipstick on my full lips and a thick layer of black mascara   on my long eyelashes in order to highlight my dark brown eyes.

I wanted to make a long eye contact with him, my thoughts started to wander, imagining myself as Virginia Hill with whom the real Bugsy Malone had fallen in love. I almost knew that movie by heart and wondered if he was as handsome as Warren Beatty. I longed for adventure, romance and long hot kisses. I heard a firm knock on my door, my heart was racing. I rushed to the door and opened it. To my surprise, he was a very good looking man. He was tall and had perfect masculine traits and his eyes had the colour of a quiet blue sea. He could have been easily mistaken for a famous model from one of those CK adverts.

"Hi, I'm Virginia Hill, "I said smiling and feeling slightly embarrassed, not knowing what he was thinking about my appearance.

"Bugsy Malone here, nice to meet you, "he answered as we both walked into the living room. He was wearing jeans and a nice expensive leather jacket which was highlighting his broad shoulders .His body was strong and muscular, his presence exuded power.

" I brought a bottle of champagne, we can have some if you like," he said, unzipping his jacket. I rushed to the kitchen and brought two champagne glasses .I filled his glass almost to the brim and reluctantly, poured very little into mine.

" Why don't you fill it to the brim like mine? "He asked with a puzzled look on his face.

" I had some liver problems and I cannot have alcohol .I'm sure that you understand." It was a lie, a white lie, but I knew that I could not take risks. I was afraid that he might want a second glass and worried that alcohol might make him aggressive. I took the half empty glass from his hand and laid it on the table.

" Shall I take the bottle and the glasses to the kitchen? " I said, looking straight into his eyes and opening my mouth slightly in the most sensuous way possible. We won't want to spill all that on the table or the carpet when we get a little wilder, don't you think so?"

" Yeah, I totally agree "he responded, touching my bum through the fabric of my dress.

He stood up and took my hands into his. I looked into his eyes and wanted that moment to last forever. His hands grabbed my waist and his eyes lingered on my breasts, moving up to my lips .I wanted him to kiss me and whisper naughty things into my ear. I wanted his body to melt into mine, I wanted him to make love to me all night long. I was overwhelmed with an incontrollable desire to surrender to all his whims.

He licked my lips and stuck his tongue into my mouth, searching for mine and sucking it gently. I felt so weak and desperately wanted him inside me.

"Kneel on the couch and let me have you that way, "he whispered.

" Just do as I say. Let me have you the way I want."

"I'm not into rough sex, "I responded, slightly worried.

"It is not rough, you will love it. I know you want me this way too."I knelt down and looked back at him.

"Do not look back at me, not until I tell you to do so, "he said in a firm voice.

He lifted my dress and torn off my panties .With a sudden movement he penetrated me deeply and started to move in and out so slowly. He reached my mouth and pushed his tongue inside it .I sucked his tongue and he pushed deeper, his hips were almost crushing mine .Rotating his hips, he moved back, allowing his penis to come out..

"I want to feel your sex, "he said, rubbing his cock against the puffy lips. I was aching inside and almost begged him to put it back. He pushed his penis deep to the root and started to move in and out frantically. I came with tears running down my cheeks and he followed me shortly.

" Turn around and look at me .You can do that now."

I stood up and smoothed my dress with my hands, looking at his naked body. To my amazement, his body was almost fully covered with tattoos.

" Can I come closer and look at them?" I asked, wondering if he was not belonging to some cult or mafia, as I spotted so many stars and religious symbols. He nodded his head in agreement.

"You have so many things tattooed on your body. Is this thing here written in Russian?"

"Do not ask me what do they mean .I'm not supposed to talk about them and I do not want to put your life in danger."

"Why did you choose me? " I inquired with a puzzled look on my face. "You could have chosen any other beautiful young girl."

"I have seen too much in my life and have been with too many women. I have been visiting prostitutes since I was 14. My father introduced them to me .I'm bored to death and I always pick up a new girl .So today I chose you."

 Sadly, I had to face the reality, my imaginary romance was over. He was not Bugsy Malone and I was not Virginia Hill.

"Did you like it? "He asked as he was moving towards the door.

"Have you not seen it? I had tears of joy running down my face, I did not want it to end .I have never felt this way before."

"I'm sure there will be many other men who will make you feel this way, "he replied, making an effort to hide that he has been taken by surprise with my remark.

A woman who longs for love...

My mobile rang at every 10 min and I almost started to hate it. I had always been a very private person and had enjoyed spending my time alone or indulging my hobbies occasionally. I started to long for those moments as I felt that all these people were invading my privacy with their incessant phone calls. This job had taken its toll on me; I could not cope up with the daily stress. I suffered from insomnia and recurrent outbursts of psoriasis .I felt drained.

I always worried about my own safety when I had to meet a new client so I made sure I chatted him long enough in order to elicit a response that might provide me with any clue in regards to ethnicity, education or job. I often felt like a detective woman who had to use her instinct when evidence was missing. Not knowing what my clients were going to look like and having only a phone number I had to use my gut feeling, relying on whatever I could derive from our conversation. It was a very risky job, I knew that I had to use my brain or I could have ended really badly.

After years of seeing myriad of clients I was terrified by the idea of having a client with a big cock and a high sex drive who would be pounding into me for an hour. I was not in my 20's anymore and my sex drive was not that high; that would have been a nightmare. I knew that I could not keep up with a stallion so I always made sure that there were at least 20 min foreplay, some oral and then sex. My body changed so much over these years , my breasts and my vagina became so sensitive , I could not stand too much nipple stimulation and I did my best to dissuade men from fingering my sex.

Having intercourse with different men on a daily basis had made me unresponsive to any kind of stimulation and sex had become a mechanic act. I would seldom enjoy sex. My vagina would not lubricate and even well endowed men found themselves in an embarrassing position, not being able to penetrate me without using a considerable amount of lube. In a very strange way, some of these men became very aroused seeing that they could not gain entrance to my vagina so easily, and after applying the lube they pushed so hard as if they wanted to tear the maidenhead of a virgin.

"You are so tight, it almost hurts."

 My thoughts went astray, wondering if they ever thought of me as person with feelings and emotions and not only as a body which was used for their own pleasure. I knew that I was not dead sexually, I knew that the right man could revive me. I longed for a man to love and cherish , I wanted to marry and wear a beautiful white princess dress .I never lost my hope for finding true love and during my moments of solitude I wished for that to happen.

As women we dream of love and romance and we love with our heart .We cannot define what love is, but we know when it's there. We seek stability and we want a man who would be loyal, a man who would commit to us for the rest of our lives. That's why perhaps we hesitate so much when an opportunity to cheat on our spouse presents itself. We are sensitive, protective and deeply emotional. Without these essential attributes women could not have been good wives and good mothers. Our own image about ourselves is very different from the way men picture us. Men are more instinctual and visual. We can spend hours looking for a beautiful dress and jewellery because we want to look good and we want to be admired for our taste and elegance. A man would see a beautiful body and his only wish would be for you to take it off.

Oral lessons for a gay...

I was about to exit my door that morning when the telephone rang around 9. I was in the habit of doing my grocery shopping early in the morning as I knew that sometimes people booked earlier than noon.

" I would like to book for 11 this morning if possible. "

"Sure that can be arranged. Do you have any questions, like you know, what would you like me to do?"

"No, I do not have any questions, just do what you normally do" he responded in a careless manner.

I found that strange as most of my clients were talkative and always keen to know more about the services I provided. Assuming that he was too shy to ask any questions, I agreed for 11 as he requested. Dressed up in my sexy outfit and wearing my high heel shoes I walked to the door and opened it, hoping that my appearance will make a good impression. To my surprise, he did not seem to notice it, he looked as if his mind was somewhere far away.

" Are you ok? If you changed your mind and want to leave that's fine with me. It is a free country."

"No, I'm fine, "he answered in the same careless manner. We walked to the bedroom and I started to undress, urging him to do the same.

"Keep your clothes on," he said, taking his jacket and his pants off.

"Are you not going to take your underwear off?" I asked puzzled, noticing the vacant look in his eyes.

" Yes, I do it now," he replied, staring at the wall and ignoring my presence completely. Not wanting to put up with all that nonsense and being slightly irritated by his demeanour, I stood up and moved towards him.

"Don't touch me, "he said as I tried to take his hands into mine." "I'm gay, "he continued in a low voice.

"Then, what can I do for you?" I responded, shocked and almost lost for words.

"I want you to teach me about oral sex. I want to work as gay escort."

"Ok, I can do that for you. Please lie down on the bed, "I answered, moving my hands towards his penis.

"No, you can't touch .I don't like it. "

"But I will have to put my mouth there if you want me to teach you about oral sex, "I responded, outraged by his whole attitude.

"Bring me my jacket, I will show you."

Sliding his hand into one of the pockets he pulled out a pink vibrator made of soft rubber which resembled an almost 6 inches penis with a considerable girth and balls.

" Take it in your hand and show me, "he urged me. " Show me everything I need to know." All of a sudden I felt relieved and all my fears were now gone.

"Why did you not ask me about this when we spoke earlier? "I inquired, wanting to know the real reason for his silence.

"I was afraid that you might say no or maybe you thought that I was joking."

"Well, you did just the right thing. I might have said no for sure as no other gay men had ever called me before to inquire about my services, "I responded smiling.

"I will show you how to give a hand job first and then I will teach you everything about giving best oral stimulation to a man."

I showed him all my tricks and asked him to do it himself, and to my surprise he proved to be extremely good at it.

"Remember, "I said, looking straight into his eyes."No teeth, remember that. Never use your teeth that might put some men off completely."

I was very good at it myself and showed him my special technique with an amazing twist which had become quite an addiction for most of my regular clients. He seemed to be very pleased with my lessons and became more talkative during our session.

" Where can I advertise for this?" he asked, trying to make eye contact.

"I know very little about gay escorts, but I'm sure there are websites where gay escorts advertise for their services. You know that some gay men will ask for anal, did you ever have that?"

"No, never did, "he responded with a surprised look on his face. " I did only oral with my gay friends, never tried anal."

"I have a strap on and I can try that with you. You have to get used to anal sex as most of the gay men will ask for that."

I looked at his skinny body and felt sorry that he had to undergo the pain and discomfort of first anal penetration.

"Yes, do that! "He urged me, kneeling on the bed submissively.

" I will be very gentle, do not worry, but remember that some might have a very large penis and they might be quite aggressive. You will have to use a dildo everyday to stretch there as you are very tight." Using my strap on, I managed to penetrate him half and not wanting to really hurt him I asked if we should stop.

"Yes, it is very painful .We must stop for now." He put his clothes on and thanked me for my patience and for being his best teacher.

" I hope I did not hurt you .Do not forget to use a dildo everyday or you might have to put up with an unbearable pain." I was more than satisfied with our meeting as it was the first time when I earned good money without having to take my clothes off and without having to share my body with strangers.

"If I could teach all women my special techniques with that amazing twist they would have had better relationships and marriages, ", I thought to myself smiling.

I had fantasised often about making love to a woman and hoped that one day I will have a chance to put my naughty ideas into practice.

Making love to a good wife...

In a strange way I started to become more attracted to women than to men, the simple thought of a young, beautiful woman exposing those soft puffy lips made me wet and full of desire.

Not being able to achieve sexual satisfaction with my clients anymore I started to watch lesbian porn videos on a daily basis, playing with my toys and offering myself the most intense orgasms. I almost started to develop an obsession for young, curvy women with a lovely fit body, a nice bum and big breasts. I became attracted to the idea of participating into orgies with groups of women and masturbated too many time fantasizing about a threesome, imagining two beautiful women sharing my body and kissing and caressing every inch of it. I liked them fully shaved there and the thought of a woman rubbing those soft puffy lips against my pussy lips made me wild with desire. I knew that I was not a lesbian and my attraction to women must have been triggered by my lack of interest in men as I have been sleeping with too many.

It was a lovely sunny day and I decided to go out for a walk, hoping that nobody was going to call and book an appointment. I really wanted to spend some time outdoors. I loved to sit on a bench and look at people passing by, trying to read their faces and wondering what their life was like. I must have been sitting there in the park for more than twenty minutes when my mobile rang. I answered the phone reluctantly as I would have liked to spend the entire afternoon outdoors, knowing that such days were rare in London.

" Hi there, I was wondering if you see couples. My wife saw your picture and she liked it very much. She wants to have sex with a woman, it would be her first time."

"I'm very much interested as it would be my first time as well, "I answered, excited by the prospect of making my fantasy real.

"Would you like to participate in or you just want to look at us while we play with each other? "I asked as it would have been my first threesome.

" I'm not quite sure as we never did this before .I might find it hard to only stay aside and watch .I would probably want to touch my wife and I need to know If I'm allowed to touch you, " he answered , laughing .

"I would like to see a picture of her first if you do not mind, I asked, knowing that I would have politely declined if she were not my type.

" Yes, no problem, I will do that right now."

She looked stunning, she was young and curvy and very fit. I was very excited to meet her, but I wanted us to be alone. It would have been my first experience with a woman and I would not have liked to be spoiled by the presence of a man.

" Your wife looks amazing, she is just my type. I can offer you a discount if I can be with your wife only. I hope that you do not mind. Please ask her and let me know what your decision is. I would like her to be fully shaved there, that can be a real turn on for me."

"I will call you back, "he replied politely, not seeming to be bothered with my question. I resumed my seat on the bench and began to fantasize about meeting his wife, wondering how she would be in person. The loud dial tone of my mobile brought me up to reality.

"Hi there, we spoke earlier about you and my wife. She agreed and I agreed too. I hope you two are going to have a great time. Can you see her at 7 tonight?"

" Yes, I can see her at 7. I look forward to meeting her then. I shall text you my address shortly, "I answered with my heart racing.

It was almost 3 o'clock and though I had plenty of time to prepare myself, I started to grow anxious about our meeting, worrying that we might not raise to each other expectations .I decided to go straight home, hoping that nobody else was going to book that afternoon as I wanted to save all my energy for the evening. I took a long bath and made sure that I was smooth like a baby. She was at my door at 7 sharp. My heart was beating wildly and I struggled to compose myself.

" Hi, I'm Sarah .You smell so good, "she said, kissing my cheeks.
"

"I'm Val, nice to meet you .That picture did not do you justice, you look much better in person." She was wearing a short tight black dress and high heel suede sandals.

" Please have a seat on the couch in the living room .I'm going to bring some strawberries. I will be with you shortly."

" Thank You .That would be very nice. ".I returned with a bowl full of big ripe strawberries.

" You look great in this lovely red dress , it goes great with your complexion and your dark hair, " she said , looking at me and smiling as I sat on the couch next to her .Her attitude was very encouraging, she was very warm and friendly .

" You know that I have never been with a woman before and never expected a woman to book a session with me. I'm just curious, sorry I do not wish to pry, but what prompted you to act this way?" I asked, touching her hand gently.

" Do not worry, have nothing to hide , I will explain everything .My husband and I stopped having sex four years ago when he was diagnosed with prostate cancer and had to undergo surgery."

"Sorry to interrupt you, but I really could not imagine that, I mean I never thought of prostate cancer .Does that affect a man's sex drive?" I asked, slightly worried that my question was inappropriate.

" Yes, it does .He can have erection if I stimulate him orally, but sex would be impossible as it does not last .He can have orgasm though he said that it did not feel like before."

" I'm sorry to hear that, but it must have been very difficult for you not to have sex these years .Have you ever thought of ending your marriage?" I asked frowning, thinking that she was too young to deny herself the pleasure of intercourse.

"You know, I thought of that, but I do love my husband. We had the best sex before and that helps a lot now. I play with my toys on a regular basis and fantasize about those moments in order to make myself come. I could not have sex with another man, it would have been a mechanic act. I can be sexually fulfilled only with the man I love .I know that it might sound strange to you, "she replied, looking at me as if she was anxious for my response.

"I'm not surprised with that at all, "I replied, knowing how much truth was in her remark.

We looked at each other slightly embarrassed, not knowing how we were going to proceed, wondering who was going to take the first step and break the ice. I kissed her, her lips were soft and sweet .She stuck her tongue into my mouth, making me moan softly. I touched her breasts through the fabric of her dress.

" Oh that feels so good, to be touched like that after such a long time. "

" What do you mean? Your husband did not touch you like this?" I asked softly, looking into her eyes.

"No, he did not touch me like this, you do not understand .He did not lose only his erection in terms of duration, he also lost the desire. I could have walked naked in front of him and he would not care. I found that very hard," she said with a tremor in her voice, almost on the brink of breaking into tears.

I commiserated with all her pain and disappointment and wanted somehow to make up for it. I wanted to make love to her in the sweetest way possible .I kissed her lips and neck and nibbled at her ear lobe.

" Please unzip my dress and take it off .I cannot bear it anymore! "She urged me in a beseeching voice.

 Her naked body was gorgeous, her skin was soft and her breasts were big and lovely .I wanted to bury my face into them, I wanted to feel the scent of her body. I took my dress off and removed my bra and my panties.

"Let's go to the bedroom, we need room. I have a king size bed there. "

She stood up and walked first, wearing nothing except for her black underwear. Her body was strikingly beautiful and I found myself craving every inch of it. I wondered what a man would have felt like to be in the company of such heavenly creature. Her voluptuous body was perfect, she had the right curves in the right places .I sat on the bed and urged her to come close to me so that my eyes could feast on her beautiful curves.

" Take your bra off, I want to see your lovely breasts! "I said to her, wanting to make love to her slowly, not caring too much about the time.

Taking her bra off, she came closer to me and started to move her hands through my hair, running her fingers down my cheeks and to my lips, making me moan with desire. My hands searched for her nipples and rubbed them gently with the tip of my fingers until they almost doubled in size .I felt an uncontrollable desire to rub my breasts against hers, I wanted to lick her hard nipples and make her beg for more.

" Lie on the bed with me Sarah, lie on the bed and relax! "I whispered to her in a low voice. I kissed her passionately and licked and sucked her hard nipples and then rubbed them against mine.

" Spread your legs Sarah, let me see that flower, "I said to her, noticing that she started to wriggle her hips lightly. She was so beautiful there, her sex was like a pink rose in full bloom.

" What a big difference is between a naked man and a naked woman!" I thought to myself.

A woman's body was far more beautiful and more sensuous than a man's naked body. I kissed her puffy lips and explored her vagina with my tongue, tormenting her with pleasure and making her moan loudly.

" I want to play with your body Val. Come, lie down next to me. I want to smell and taste your body. "

Aroused by her passionate words I lay next to her, delighted to be at her mercy. She kissed and caressed my body , driving me wild with pleasure and making me beg her to stop tormenting me like that .Her mouth and hands were so skilful as if she instinctively knew where and how to touch. How different was this from all my experiences with men who were often clumsy and selfish , paying so little attention to foreplay and rushing to achieve their own pleasure .For most of my clients the foreplay was reduced more or less to an attempt to emulate the behaviour of men from the porn videos they watched.

Pornography has spoiled the ability to act spontaneously and to relate to a woman in the most natural way possible. Pornography has nothing to do with love; pornography is about penetration and close up where even the smallest cock can look huge. I do not think that all men become addicted to pornography, but I do believe that watching porn on a daily basis could do a lot of harm by poisoning the minds of men with unrealistic ideas and expectations in regards to sex.

 Pornography is an act and those people are paid to perform sex scenes which in real life could not be possible. Sex can be a very exhausting activity for both men and women and perhaps more for men in terms of duration and performance. In the real world where we live such busy lives performing sexually to that level would be physically impossible.

 I stopped watching any lesbian porn videos, I found them boring and aggressive after my experience with Sarah. I realized that those lesbian porn videos were made for men and not for women. Sarah and I acted as naturally as possible without following any cliché/scenario created by an industry whose main purpose is to cater to men's taste.

 There was no need for dirty talk and bottom slapping and we did not have to use any huge rubber dildos to insert into our vaginas or anuses in order to please each other sexually. We both knew that we were not lesbians and I think we were both trying to replace sexual dissatisfaction with a lesbian experience. We must have spent more than two hours together and she generously offered to pay for my extra time. I could not accept it and I declined politely, delighted to have been in the company of such a lady .She was sensitive and caring and she loved her husband. I kissed her and hugged her tightly when we parted and wished her my very best.

A young man seeking advice...

To my surprise some of the very young men who came to see me did not display any immediate interest in sex .Their behaviour was totally different from the demeanour of my usual clients who were usually very chatty and could not keep their hands away from me, wanting me to dispose of my clothes as soon as possible.

" Are you ok sweetheart? " I asked the tall athletic guy who came to see me that morning, noticing that he was unusually quiet once he entered my room.

" I'm fine thanks, "he answered, looking down at the floor and sighing.

"Take a seat on the couch and make yourself comfortable. Would you like a glass of cold water?"

"Yes, that would be very nice as I'm quite thirsty, "he replied, staring at me with piercing eyes.

"Here it is, your glass of water, "I said, handing the glass to him. He laid his mobile on the bed and took the glass from my hand. He gulped the water down his throat, emptying it in seconds.

"Thanks, I was really thirsty, "he said smiling."

"It is my pleasure sweetheart .Now tell me what can I do for you?" I replied, taking a seat on the bed near him.

Slightly embarrassed with my question and my very close presence, he moved few inches away.

" You know, I'm not here for sex .I need to talk to you, I need your advice. "

" You can confide all your secrets to me, feel free to disburden your heart .I'm a good listener and I hope that I will be able to give you some good advice, "I responded, taken by surprise with his request.

"You are a woman and I'm sure that you understand women better than I do. I have been working as a door supervisor in Spain at a night club during the summer and fell in love with one of the girls who worked as a stripper .I returned to London a week ago and she stopped answering my phone calls and I do not know what do to. I miss her so much."

I could sense pain and disappointment in his voice and somehow I could not understand it myself. He was a very handsome young man, his body was strong and very fit.

" You look so good and your body is perfect. Have you ever been to bodybuilding contests? "I inquired, deliberately digressing from our topic.

It was part of my strategy to distract people with more positive things in order to cheer them up or at least make them forget about their sadness temporarily.

" Oh yes, I have been to several contests in the past .But I needed money so I started to work as bodyguard for some very rich people and then later went astray and got myself into trouble."

"Why did you go to Spain? Were you not making good money working for the rich people?" I inquired slightly puzzled.

"Oh you do not know anything about working for rich people. Some of them are really nasty, you can make good money, but their behaviour is unbearable .Some of them think they are Gods and you have to cater to every whim so I quit and started to work for some big drug dealers and that's how I got myself into prison for two years. It was my mistake, but who is perfect? I just wanted to move forward."

" What did you have to do for these drug dealers? I would like some details as you have made me very curious. Everything will remain between these walls so do not worry, "I said, trying to somehow reassure him about my discretion.

"It's ok, I'm fine with that, it is past .I did not kill anybody if that is what you want to know, "he replied, bursting into a laughter.

" I was supervising the deals and had to make sure all went well. They were Croatians and the drugs were brought by other guys from Montenegro .Part of my job was to check if the drugs were genuine and had to weigh every bag in their presence .That was extremely stressful, you know how these guys are, they have a volatile disposition. They could have shot me for the very simple reason that they did not like my face anymore ".

I found myself immersed in his story.

" So how did you end up in prison then?" I asked, wanting to know more about his adventurous past.

"You must have seen this stuff in the movies, you know that it always ends badly in one way or another. Somehow information leaked to the police and we were caught in the middle of the action .It must have been one of their friends who worked as intelligence for the police. It could not have been any of my friends as I did not have too many and the few ones did not know about what I was doing. "

" Being in prison for two years must have been very hard. You do not look like a bad guy at all, I think you were under some bad influence and you were lured by easy money."

" Yes, that is true, but I do not regret anything .All that helped me grow up, "he replied in a more optimistic tone, slightly surprised with my remark.

" Are you going to go back to Spain or you found work here in London? I asked, seeing that almost thirty minutes of our time had passed and not wanting to waste more time I turned the conversation to our initial topic.

"Yes, I found good job here as door supervisor for night clubs and private parties. I shall go to Spain again in the summer, "he responded in a low voice. Noticing some kind of bitterness in his response I was determined to be as frank as I could, hoping to put some sense into his mind.

"You know, that girl in Spain, she worked as a stripper right? Our jobs are somehow similar, we cannot allow ourselves to fall in love or commit to a long term relationship. That would interfere with our work and it always ends badly.You know that men are jealous, I mean most of them .I heard that some men like to watch their wives having sex with another men and that is something I could never understand."

"I was not looking for commitment, I just want to understand why she stopped answering my phone calls," he said, inhaling and exhaling deeply.

"Do you love her? " I asked, wanting to understand his feelings better.

"I do not know if I love her, but I definitely miss her. We had such a great time there. "

" I cannot foresee the future, but you either forget about her or you go to Spain and find out for yourself. She might have stopped answering your phone call because she realized that she could not get involved in a serious relationship .I do not think that she found any fault with you physically , you look very good. I doubt that there is another man, however you are the only one to discover the truth. I offered you an explanation from my point of view as a woman and escort girl, but it does not mean that is the truth. "

"That's fine, I understand. Thank You for your advice and your time .By the way, what's the time?"

"Well, we still have almost 20 min left so what do you suggest?" I asked smiling.

"You know I did not come here for sex .I'm not in the mood to go with a woman, but it would be nice to have some relief .So why do not take off your clothes so that I can look at your body while I rub my cock? I have a fetish for nice strong legs and big bum and you just look like that. I'm going to lie down on the bed , you just stand up on the bed with your back towards me so that I can see you better " he urged me , taking his pants off .

I looked in the mirror which was on the opposite wall on my right hand side and noticed the cellulite on my bum and legs.

" You have strong legs and your bottom looks amazing "he whispered, rubbing his cock.

He did not seem to be bothered with my cellulite and I wondered if he noticed it at all. I always had my insecurities about my own body, but it became almost an obsession once I started to work as an escort. I knew I was not very young anymore and I had to compete with thousands of girls who advertised for their services, girls who were younger and slimmer and more attractive .I hated diets and my time was limited, I could not afford to spend hours in the gym every day.

Despite all my concerns almost all of my clients complimented me on my good looks and that has been a great help in terms of boosting my own self-confidence. It must have been the way I dressed up and that was something I have always been very particular about. I knew that a slovenly appearance would not have brought me too many clients so I always made sure that my appearance was impeccable from head to toe.

"It was very nice meeting you, "he said, wiping himself and looking for his clothes.

"I hope that you and your girl get back together and if that does not happen remember that there is plenty of fish in the pond .You are a handsome guy so no worries," I replied, starting to dress up.

Shared by two young boys...

It started to rain heavily that morning and wondered how my day was going to be like .I could not function without my morning fix of caffeine so put my kettle to boil and turned on my laptop. I did most of my shopping online and that morning I wanted to buy some new toys and some wet look outfits. Wet look clothing can turn on a man instantly, I knew that men were very visual and my clients loved them. My telephone rang and I smiled to myself, thinking that one could not have been taken by surprise with too many bookings on such a boring day.

" Hi, it's me the guy with the mommy role play. I want to see you today, but not for our usual role play. I want to come with my friend so you can have two boys. "I have never been with two men before, but I had fantasized about it. I was excited by the idea of sharing my body with two young, inexperienced boys.

" Well, tell me about your friend first, is he nice and well-mannered like you?" I asked, needing some reassurance from him as my safety always came first. I was not interested in a hard core experience or rough sex, I wanted an erotic experience.

"Oh yes, do not worry. He is like me, nice and young boy. He has never been with an escort girl and I want to introduce him to you. He might be too shy to play with you, but he will enjoy watching, I'm sure."

"I can do that, yes .What time shall we make it? " I asked anxiously, pleased with his answer and looking forward to see them both.

"The sooner we meet the better, so in one hour? Would that be ok?"

"Yes, see you at 11. We will have a great time ".

I was excited to meet them both and wanted to make the most of it, knowing that it could have been my first and my last experience with two men .I took a long shower and dressed up as sexy as I could, choosing a pair of wet look high heel boots and a lovely black sheer body suit .I rushed to the door to open it.

" Hi, both very punctual .I like that .Please come in, we will have a little chat first .Then we can go to the bedroom and have great fun ".

I wanted to make sure that they understood my rules.

" I do not want anything aggressive so you just do what I ask for .I'm sure that you are both going to like it, "I said while my eyes were sizing up his friend .He was short and skinny and he seemed to be completely absorbed with the sight of my breasts .

" You like them? You can touch them "I asked, moving closer to him.

"Wow! They are so big, they look amazing .Are they real or you have implants?" he asked with a surprised look on his face.

"Yes, they are real and you will be playing with them soon .Let's not waste any more time so follow me to the bedroom."

I knelt down on the wooden floor and asked them to stand up in front of me .I unzipped their pants and released both cocks from the pressure of the underwear. I started to lick and suck both cocks at the same time until they grew so big that my mouth could not accommodate them. I spit on them and started to rub them in my hands, urging both of them to touch my breasts and play with my nipples.

"Oh my God, this is amazing .Oh look at you, please take your top off .We want to see your boobs," said the little one in a trembling voice.

I stood up and took my top off , kissing each of them passionately .They started to lick and suck my nipples driving me wild with desire and making me moan loudly .I knelt down and licked and sucked their cocks one by one, rubbing them both against my erect nipples .

" Oh God, that is too much .I do not want to come now so I will step aside. I will just watch both of you play. "

"You just stand up at the edge of the bed and look at us. Mommy and I are going to play, "said the mommy fantasy guy as we both moved towards the bed.

" Come on top of me and put that cock all over my face, rub it against my mouth lips and put it inside my greedy mouth, "I said ,determined to drive his friend crazy , knowing that he was watching us without blinking.

" Oh Baby you suck so good, your mouth is amazing .Take it deeper baby, deeper just like that...I'm coming baby, I'm coming ..."

Lying on the bed with my face covered in semen I looked at his friend and asked if he would like to try the same. I must have looked like one of those women from the porn movies.

" Yes, suck me, I want the same like him."

He put his cock in my mouth and came in seconds.

" I need a towel and I think you need one too, "I said, pointing to the bathroom.

Nauseated by the pungent smell of his semen I wiped my face thoroughly and reached for my silk dressing gown which was hanging next to my bed.

" You know, that was my first blow job. He told me that you were the best. Your mouth was so soft, I did not feel any teeth at all" he said in the most sincere way, with an innocent face that reminded me of a child.

I was more than happy to hear it, knowing that what had happened between us would stick with him for a long time. They were both two young and well-mannered boys who just wanted to try something new and it must have been my friendly nature that prompted my regular client to bring his friend. We both enjoyed seeing his curious looks and his excitement which somehow brought up memories from the past when we experienced things for the first time. I threw my silk gown on the bed and jumped into the shower. I felt exhausted and wondered if I could have enough energy for my next client.

Are you married?

"Are you married?" It was the question that some of my clients would ask as soon as they would have met me.

" Why do you think I should be married?" I retorted with a fake smile, trying to conceal my irritation.

I resented that question and wondered if it was not perhaps because all of a sudden it reminded me of the mistakes I made in my life. It was my cowardice and my selfishness that made me choose the other side, depriving myself of one of the greatest and noble role, to be a good wife and a good mother. I chose career to motherhood and family and now I found myself to have gone astray from my initial goal and from my moral principles.

 I felt that I had lost both. My life was now filled with regrets and in a hopeless way I tried to replace them with an expensive lifestyle which was so unsuitable to my own nature. I was a modest good-natured village girl who had been brought up into a very good family with strong morals and principles. My heart had been corrupted by easy money. I lived a life which most of my female friends would most likely covet and yet I was so unhappy. My life was lacking spirituality .I owned things and sadly, they were just things, expensive clothes and jewellery and perfumes.

 I had become addicted to my lifestyle and despite that I loathed the constant invasion of my privacy I could not stand to be alone for long periods of time. I craved the attention of my clients and loved the compliments on my good looks .I often experienced withdrawal symptoms when circumstances would prevent me from attending my daily job. I almost started to hate my period and anything that might have kept me away from my work.

Strangely, some men would phone me soon after our meeting or many days after, trying unsuccessfully to coax me to go out with them, inviting me to movies or expensive restaurants.

" You are such an attractive woman, why don't you come out with me and have a nice dinner and a drink? I like you very much and that would be very nice."

 I had the unpleasant task to decline politely and even resort to more drastic measures when a NO could not be taken for a NO , adding their numbers to my very long black list so that they could not reach me. I often wondered if there was any semblance of truth in their words or maybe they just wanted to obtain more than a paid session from me.

 "They could not have been under the spell of my appearance, "I thought to myself.

 I considered myself pretty average so it must have been those sexy outfits and my friendly nature that prompted them to act in such a childish manner or maybe loneliness or a desperate attempt to obtain some sexual favours free of charge. I found it more puzzling when such an invitation came from a former client who was divorced and had three children in his care.

 "I have my children with me, my marriage did not work out unfortunately .But they are three bright kids and I love them. Look at these pictures, are they not nice?" he asked anxious to see my reaction."

 "Life can be such an unfair game "I thought to myself, it was either win or lose, like lottery.

 I wondered what could have gone wrong about their marriage as they have been blessed to have three beautiful and healthy children. Why are not people aware of the ups and downs when they vow to each other everlasting love? We fall in love with our hearts and unprepared for whatever is to come in our way we give up too easily and often make the wrong decision when we face an obstacle. I think people have unrealistic expectations in the beginning of their marriages and that is why so marriages fail. It is an almost impossible task to keep the balance even when we are constantly harassed by daily challenges.

" Yes , they look lovely and you must be very proud of them," I responded more than willing to change the subject , suddenly overwhelmed with the imaginary burden of having to be the mother of the three children.

I wanted exclusivity in a relationship and could not see myself dating a man with three children who probably needed most of his presence and attention.

"Why don't you come out with me this week end? We can go somewhere and have nice food and drinks and maybe if we get along well we can go more often. What do you think?" he asked with piercing eyes. Aware that I had to choose my words carefully, I smiled back to him and declined his invitation in the most polite way possible.

" You know, I do not mix business with pleasure, I do not go out with my clients. You are not the only person who asked me and you know that I'm here and you are here, and once you exit that door you face reality."

I paused for a moment to catch my breath and then continued.

" I'm an ordinary person in real life and you will get bored with me in less than a week, believe me, "I said in the most convincing tone, hoping to dissuade him from proposing anything like that in the future.

Laying his hands on my shoulders, he looked into my eyes and nodded his head in agreement.

"Fair enough, I understand what do you mean, it makes sense. I appreciate your good intentions and your sincerity. So let's not waste any more time and have great fun then."

A much needed change...

To my surprise some men were not interested in sex at all and they would make it very clear to me on the phone before I opened my mouth to continue the conversation.

" I'm not looking for sex at all, I just want a nice sensual massage and 69."

"That works very well with me so just let me know what time you can make it, "I responded, pretending to be pleased with their request.

I was not a very slim young girl anymore and a 69 was more of a burden than anything pleasant. I usually accepted such bookings only when I had a poor week and knew that lack of clients meant less money which I dreaded. My joins were aching and to my embarrassment I often had to stop in the middle of the session overwhelmed by the excruciating pain of a sudden cramp .My clients did not seem to be bothered very much with my apologies and they eagerly encouraged me to resume my position, not wanting to waste any time with idle talk.

"I want to make you come" they whispered to me with their faces buried into my pussy, while their tongues were lapping my clit and my vagina.

 Faking an orgasm and moaning as loud as I could was the best way to hasten their climax and put an end to all my nightmare After five years of being used constantly almost every day, my body had become very sensitive to touching , especially my nipples and my vagina. I would often suffer from great discomfort in my genital area as a consequence or oral sex and too much fingering so I tried to avoid oral sex as much as I could and fingering was totally forbidden .Most men, except for very few, had little knowledge about pleasing a woman orally and their aggressive fingering caused me more pain than pleasure. I always explained to them in the most polite way that faster does not necessarily mean better and that unlike those women from the porn movies, in real life most women would prefer a fast but gentle fingering.

 I liked to be in control with my clients so the more pliable they were the better and to my great surprise some of them were more than pliable. They would just simply lie down on the bed without asking anything and quietly enjoying the pleasure they received from my skilful mouth. I wished all my clients were that way, to have them lying down at my mercy was an ideal situation as they would more likely keep their hands away from my body.

 I stopped advertising for full service as I felt that my body needed a long break to recover so I started to advertise for massage and light domination which had brought me plenty of clients though not as many as I hoped for. Despite that I had to charge less I was happy to compromise for a while and give up temporarily to my expensive shopping habits. Massages with happy ending were very popular and happy ending meant rather a good blow job as most of the prospective client's preferred oral relief to hand relief.

"How many times I can come in one hour?" It was the kind of question I abhorred most.

"Well, you can come to my place as many times as you like in one hour "I replied ironically, knowing exactly what they meant by that.

 To me that was the most insulting thing, I was a human being and not a glory hole. Annoying situations required drastic measures and blocking their numbers was the best solution to my problem.

"Do you do oral with or without condom?" That was the type of question I resented less as it was more justifiable in terms of one's safety.

 " Well, it depends on how much you care about your own safety .I'm fine with both, but if I were in your place I would not risk ," I answered in the most convincing tone , trying to persuade them to choose in favour of a condom every time.

The light domination service proved to be quite funny despite that in the beginning I was not very pleased with the idea. I started to enjoy inflicting light pain and discovered that it was quite a stress relief therapy for me. The best thing about working as an escort girl is undoubtedly the spontaneity of the situations; you could never get bored with your job. I could not see myself as a real dominatrix who would probably have a well equipped den and very likely would be skinny and dressed up in a latex or PVC outfit.

 Not wanting to disappoint my client's expectations and knowing that I had to keep up with the demands in the department I purchased a latex short dress and garter belt and stockings along with long latex gloves and a PVC cat suit. After cursing and sweating for about 20 min,

I managed to dress up in my latex outfit. It felt so tight on my body and so uncomfortable that I could not see myself wearing it for an hour and certainly not on a very warm day. I looked in the mirror to see what my body looked like in that very tight outfit.

 The latex looked very shiny and exciting, but it did not flatter my body at all. That outfit made me look like a sausage and my boobs and bottom were about to burst out of the tight latex. You had to be very skinny to look well in latex so I decided to wear only my latex garter belt and stockings during my light domination sessions, which were slightly more comfortable than the entire latex outfit.

Shoe lace, lady's panties and poppers

"Hi there, do you have poppers?" asked the man with a very English accent.

"I do not know what those are, "I responded, not having the slightest clue about what poppers were.

"It is something that you sniff and makes you go a little high, enhancing your pleasure."

"I'm sorry but I do not sell drugs, I'm not into that, "I replied in a firm voice.

" Let me explain it to you, it is not a drug .They sell it as a room fragrance, but if you sniff it during sex or any kind of sexual stimulation it enhances the pleasure. Do not worry I will buy it and bring it with me. I want oral stimulation and light ball torture and please wear something kinky for me. Can I see you in an hour?"

"Yes, sure I will text you the address," I responded, still puzzled with his unusual request. I had no clue what cock or balls torture was so I surfed the internet hoping to find some videos and to my surprise there were far too many. To me some of these videos looked pretty disgusting and the one where the man had his penis covered with pegs made me burst into laughter. I could not believe that people would go so far and do all these crazy things. Cock torture and balls torture sounded totally insane as I could not understand why a man would want to feel pain there; in my mind the balls were as sensitive as my breasts.

I dressed up as kinky as I could , wearing a lovely black lace top and latex garter belt and stockings, along with a pair of high heel shoes .He entered the room and walked straight to the couch in the living room , seeming to be in a hurry.

"Would you like to go to the bedroom or do you prefer to stay here?" I asked, sizing him up from head to toe.

He was dressed up in a very expensive suit and and shoes which made me think that he must have had a very well paid job and must have been working in an office for one of those big companies.

"No, we can stay here. It is my lunch break and I have to be back to office in an hour, "he responded, taking his shoes and trousers off.

He was wearing white lace panties which he must have bought from a lingerie shop or he must have taken it from his wife's wardrobe .I was shocked. That was something I really did not expect to see from a man dressed up in such a posh outfit.

"Why are you wearing lady's underwear? " I asked, looking at him with wide eyes.

"Why are you so surprised?" he answered, raising his brows.

"I do not know how to explain it to you, but I really did not expect this. Do not misunderstand me I like the idea, but seeing you dressed up in that posh outfit and wearing lady's white lace panties, that was quite something. I must admit that it looks pretty good on you, "I answered with a smile.

" I like to wear my wife's underwear, she knows about and she is very excited with this. Come, touch my cock through the lace, "he urged me, taking my hand into his and placing it over his erected penis.

To my amazement I really liked the feel of it through the lace which had become quite wet with so much pre cum. Looking at his face, I ran my fingers across his penis and his balls. His eyes were closed and he breathed heavily.

"Enough of that, do you have a ball ring? "he asked, while his hand slid into the pocket of his coat, pulling out what appeared to be a very small dark bottle.

"I'm sorry, I do not have one, I'm quite new to this stuff," I responded slightly embarrassed, hoping that he would not be too disappointed and cancel the booking.

"That's fine with me, "he answered in a calm voice.

"You can use one of my shoe laces "he said, pointing to the shoes which were not far from me.

"Yes, take the shoe lace out "he continued as I extended my hand to grab one of his shoes.

"What do you want me to do with the lace? " I asked with what I think it was one of the most puzzled look on my face.

I was expecting him to become angry with my clumsiness, but he seemed pretty calm.

" Just tie up the lace the around the balls and make a knot so that it would not loosen up. Do it as hard as you can and do not worry, I will tell you when to stop," he said, sitting down on the couch.

I knelt down in front of him and did what I was told to do.

"Tighter, tighter, "he whispered in a raspy voice, sniffing from the little dark glass bottle.

His balls turned from dark red to blue and I began to worry that he might die there and I could get myself into serious trouble.

"Are you ok? Your balls are almost black, "I asked looking at his face and wanting to hear some kind of reassurance so that my mind would be at ease.

"Yes, I'm fine, just make a tight knot and make sure you can untie it. You better start to suck my cock as time flies and I have to go back soon "he said, propping a cushion under his lower back.

He was not circumcised and his cock looked like a sausage and with his balls turning black it was quite a scary sight for an uninitiated like me. I was just silently praying that all would end up well. I started to suck him, taking his cock as deep as I could. He seemed to be completely under the spell of the vapours from his magic glass bottle. His breath quickened and his head started to flop back and forth as if he was about to collapse. I took a napkin in my hand and spit out his semen which was so bitter and had such a pungent smell that is made my stomach retch. Awoke from his state of complete trance he urged me to untie the lace as quickly as I could. His balls were still black when he slipped on his trousers.

"Are you not going to put your lace panties on?" I asked puzzled.

"No, I have another in one of my drawers at the office. And besides this needs to be washed so better without, "he replied with a grin on his face, stuffing the panties into his trouser pocket and bending to do the lace of his shoes.

He rushed to the door in a nonchalant manner and seemed to be completely detached emotionally from whatever had taken place between us minutes ago. Still under the influence of the fresh events and slightly shocked , I was amazed with his ability to suddenly shift into a different mood as if he closed a door and opened another one, without looking back.

Bite hard

"Bite my balls, bite harder. I will tell you when to stop, "said the young man in a guttural voice, not seeming to be very pleased with my shy attempt.

"I want to be your slave so treat me like one. I want to worship you, "he said, looking at me and kneeling down.

" You should start with kissing my boots, "I replied, smacking his back with my leather crop.

"No, not like that, you are totally useless .Do it slowly, slowly, lick my boots up to my knee, I whispered , poking with my crop at his cheek , pretending to be upset with his clumsiness.

"Yes mistress, yes mistress, "he responded, eager to meet my demands.

" Yes, like that, slowly, slowly, "I replied, averting my head and trying not to let him see that I was about to burst into a laughter.

I simply could not understand why such a handsome boy like him would like to be treated that way. He complied with every request and seemed to be completely absorbed with what I was doing. All of a sudden he stood up without making any eye contact and looked as if he were in a trance.

"Bite my balls hard, "he said, rubbing his cock with his hand. I bit his balls as hard as I could, look up at him to see if he was still alive.

" Bite my cock hard, "he urged me, pulling my hair lightly.

His cock felt like steel under my teeth and seemed to grow bigger and bigger as I bit harder and harder.

"Bring the latex glove you wore in that picture on your ad .Put some lube on it and rub my cock, "he said hoarsely.

I poured plenty of lube on my glove and started to rub his massive cock.

"Bite my balls and rub my cock hard, "he urged me, panting. Groaning like a wild beast he came violently, his white creamy semen dripping over my hair and my face.

" That was so good .Now I can go back to my job happy, "he said, grinning and reaching for the napkin box.

It seemed that the pain had some kind of therapeutic effect on him; his face looked so composed and his eyes were sparkling, showing a very different man from the one I looked at minutes ago.

A strap on...

"Do you have a strap on? I want you to tie me up and use that on me. I will be driving so I can be there in 30 min," said the man who must have been in his 50's.

I simply could not comprehend why a man would be interested in being fucked from behind by a woman with a fake penis. I knew that most men would not say no to anal gentle play, but the monster fake penis was something different. I motioned him to the bedroom and told him to wait a few minutes as I had to bring and fasten my strap on. He was very tall and slightly overweight and had a set of white perfect teeth. I wondered if they were real or maybe he had implants or a very nice and expensive denture. He took his clothes off and sized me up from head to toe, his eyes lingering on the huge rubber penis. His cock was limp and not as big as I expected from a person who had the body of a giant.

"Would not this be too big for you? " I asked frowning, thinking that I might hurt him.

" I'm used to big ones, do not worry so let's not waste time. Kneel down and suck me a little bit, make me heard baby."

I sucked him hard and fast and his cock grew so big that my mouth could not accommodate the monster.

"Take it deeper baby, deep throat, "he whispered hoarsely with his eyes closed.

I choked and retched as I tried to take it deep to the root. He pulled my hair and pushed his penis so deep that tears were running down my cheeks and I started to struggle for air.

"It is too big and if you push it so deep I might bite it," I said, trying to catch my breath.

"That is enough baby. Tie me up to the bedstead and fuck me from behind .I shall be rubbing my cock so you just fuck my ass," he said, kneeling down on the bed with his face in the pillow and his hands stretched wide.

I tied his hands to the poles of my bedstead as tight as I could and he winced in pain.

"Is that tight enough?" I asked grinning, happy to make him suffer a little pain.

I knew that his huge cock would cause me discomfort for days when I swallowed my food. For the first time in my life I was going to fuck somebody and I was going to feel like a man in terms of role playing. I poured some lube on the monster and positioned myself close to his hips, inserting the fake penis in his back which slid in easily and deep to the root.

"Not an anal virgin, "I thought to myself as my hips started to move faster and faster.

"That's so good baby, keep moving, faster and deeper .Oh you are so good baby, just like that, "he said panting.

I started to move my hips frantically and to my surprise I found myself enjoying it so much that I did not want it to end too soon. For a few seconds I imagined what a man might have felt when he was fucking a woman from behind like that. Moaning loud and shaking he came violently, spreading his semen over my bed sheet.

"Here is some extra as I made quite a mess and sorry for that," he said, taking the money out of his wallet .We parted in the friendliest manner and he thanked me for the service.

"I like deep throat and the strap on very much, my wife does not want to hear about, "he added before he shut the door behind him.

Many of my clients loved anal play and some of them liked it rough like this .I used to say that a man is two things: his brain and his cock and later realized that I omitted the third, his ass. To keep a man happy women have to do a lot of things and that is in addition to the daily job and chores.

"Not an easy task," I thought to myself. It is hard for a woman to be sexy and horny all the time and to be willing to fulfil such fantasies.

"Do you do prostate massage?" To my surprise so many men were interested in anal play and prostate massage. It would make them achieve such a climax that they would shake for good minutes and they would call me all names.

" Oh sweetheart, my angel I'm coming, "they whispered to me while their bodies were trembling uncontrollably.

 Tapping a man's prostate lightly with the tip of the finger could offer an ecstatic experience to a man which was, accordingly to what men described to me, something totally different from ejaculation during sex.

  It was not an easy task as you had to be ambidextrous so that the finger of one hand would tap his prostate and the other hand would rub or suck his cock at the same time. I acquired such skill with practice that I became an expert in prostate massage and had more clients than I could handle.

Scratch my balls... Touch me lightly

My professional massage with happy ending was very popular and I had my regulars who had become addicted to my amazing blow job with my magic twist. They would not hesitate to praise me highly for my acquired experience and skills.

"You are the best!"

"I loved the way you licked my balls and sucked my cock!"

"This was the best blow job I ever had!"

"That was an amazing deep throat with sloppy, wet blow job!"

"You have a magic touch baby, everything about you is perfect!"

I could not be indifferent to such remarks and despite that I felt completely drained with the demands of such a job I took pride in offering the best service. I treated my clients with the utmost respect and did my best as I wanted to be very professional. I reminded myself constantly that there were thousands of girls who offered the same type of service. The secret in this job was to have my regulars as they were more reliable in terms of providing enough income in order to keep going.

 I had always compared escorting with fishing, you threw the bait and you prayed that somebody would swallow it or you could end up with no fish. No one would like to get out of bed after seeing five or six clients during the previous day and unfortunately that was often the case as I knew that the next might be very quiet. Despite the amount of exertion involved it was in a strange way emotionally rewarding as I loved to give pleasure. My clients loved to see a friendly face, someone with whom they would feel comfortable and someone to whom they would confide their deepest secrets and fantasies.

"I come here to see you because you are such a lovely girl and always so complimentary."

"You are so different from all the other girls and I used to see many. You are chatty and educated and is a pleasure to talk with you."

"I went to other places and have to tell you that girls were not friendly and welcoming and I was so stressed out that I could not have an erection. I had to leave in the middle of the session."

I realized that some men do not feel entirely comfortable when they visit such places and very likely they must have been as apprehensive as I were before a new encounter. Sometimes despite all my kindness and efforts some men could not ejaculate. Perhaps they could not leave all the stress related to personal life or work aside or maybe their bodies could not simply respond to my intense stimulation at that moment. It left a bitter taste in my mouth as I wanted my clients to climax and go happy about their business.

The summer was unusually warm for London and for two weeks I had to bear with extremely hot days .I could not manage without my talcum powder which was liberally applied all over my body including my genitals. I knew I was going to sweat profusely during my massage sessions and besides that the talcum powder made my skin soft and fragrant. I made a habit of using it every time after my shower even during the cooler days.

 I could not provide a full body deep tissue massage naked as I would not have felt comfortable with my big breasts hanging loosely when I had to use a considerable amount of exertion. I had to wear what I called my massage outfit which consisted of a tight black transparent leotard which would keep my breasts in place and which could be easily unbuttoned so that my clients would have access to my intimate parts toward the end of my massage. The most dreadful thing was waxing down and I had no choice but to put up with the pain once a month. The bush is no longer fashionable, nowadays men like to see and touch a fully shaved pussy, not to say that it makes cunnilingus more attractive.

My one hour massage session involved a good 40 minutes deep tissue massage , the rest of 20 minutes being allocated to oral stimulation or prostate massage when the case. Tony was different from all my clients who were looking for a massage with relief , he was not looking for my professional massage and he really did not care too much about what I would be wearing. He was addicted to my magic touch.

"I just want a light massage with the tip of your fingers. I love to be touched that way and you can even scratch my body lightly with your nails. Insist with the scratching on my balls, I love that very much. No worries about oral, I prefer a hand relief."

Tony was very handsome and a real gentleman, he looked very much like Robert Redford who had been one of my favourite actors. I enjoyed our session very much and I often got carried on by it and spent more than one hour engaged in the pure delight of offering such tactile pleasure. He would lie face down on my massage bed and would meekly lift his hips in order to have a pillow slid underneath .That would elevate his hips high enough so that I could have a full view and easy access to his genitals where my fingers would work their magic.

 He had a nice round bum and amazing pink round balls. I always liked to see a nice round bum and loved the sight of balls and penis from behind of a man when his hips would be elevated high enough to offer an exciting view. He started to moan lightly as the tip of my fingers sent a shiver across his spine. I poured more oil and my fingers glided all over his body, lingering on his bottom. I started to knead his cheeks, caressing the inside part of his legs and moving my deft fingers to the perineum and anus. I spread it lightly and poured warm oil inside, sliding massaging the entrance to his anus and sliding the tip of my finger inside.

 "Oh keep doing that .That is beautiful, do you hear me? That is so beautiful, "he said panting."

I started to alternate the light sensuous teasing with short breaks so that he would not get used to it and he would crave it more and more. That made him moan so loudly that I was scared my neighbours might hear it. I was delighted to see him so excited so I moved my fingers along his spine and all the way down to his balls. I scratched them gently with my short fingernails. He went berserk

"That is so beautiful. Oh God, that is so beautiful, that feeling of your nails over my balls is amazing."

"I think it is time to turn on your back," I said in a warm voice.

His penis was quite large and erect and his balls looked much bigger as if they were about to burst out. I poured oil all over it and I started to massage his balls and penis, tapping lightly the tip and the shaft where men have a very sensitive spot similar to the G spot of the women. I kept teasing and teasing, but I knew that sometimes it would take longer to climax   due to the stress related to his job.

"I think this time is going to take longer. It is ok if it does not happen, "he said in a very calm voice.

"Shh!" I whispered, putting my index against his lips.

"You think too much. Relax and let your mind drift!".

My greatest satisfaction was to see my clients having an explosive climax and Tony was no exception. I started to stroke his penis faster and faster while the other hand caressed mercilessly his balls.

"Keep doing it just like that. I'm so close .Ohhh God I'm going to come ..." he whispered in a guttural voice, his body shaking uncontrollably. I looked at his face. He looked so peaceful and relaxed.

"That was great! God I thought I would not come with all this stress I have at work, but you did it."

"It was pleasure Tony .You are a true gentleman," I answered with a broad smile.

Suck my nipples...

I was very surprised to discover that some men enjoyed nipple teasing as I would have rather expected that from a woman. I knew that some women who were very orgasmic could simply come by just having their nipples stimulated. These men had no interest in intercourse, all they wanted was a long oral stimulation and intense nipple play. They loved to finish in my mouth while my deft fingers were tugging at their erect nipples.

"I could never come during sex even with my wife. I guess women were always happy because I lasted so long, but I could climax only this way," he said, caressing my hair and my ears while his cock was deep in my mouth.

Jason was one of my regulars and I knew exactly how he wanted it. He would lie down on the bed, waiting for the pleasure, motionless and silent. I sucked his nipples gentle and then harder, making him moan with pleasure. His cock grew hard. I wetted the index fingers with my tongue and rubbed his huge, erect nipples. I started to lick his balls and his penis, teasing with long strokes and taking it in my mouth so slowly that it made him moan louder. I loved to torture him with pleasure, I had always been more of a giver than a receiver.

"Oh you are so good, you are the best baby .Just keep doing what you are doing. Suck me, suck me harder," he urged me panting.

His cock was throbbing in my mouth as if it was about to explode.

"Come here, suck my nipples hard baby .Suck them again and again and tease them with your teeth."

I was shocked to see how huge they became as a result of intense stimulation. I wetted my fingers and tugged at them, rubbing and sucking again and again. He seemed to have gone into frenzy, breathing rapidly and clenching his hands, his heart pounding. Realizing that he was unable to talk and was probably very near to climax I spat on his nipples and rubbed my fingers over , taking his penis deep in my mouth . He came violently in my mouth, his hips almost crushing my face, hurting my chin and my nose. He was lying down on the bed for a few good minutes, exhausted with such an intense climax. I went to the bathroom and washed my face, it was reddish and it hurt when I wiped my chin and my nose.

"No Pain, no gain, "I thought to myself, forcing a smile.

"That was mind blowing, thank you. I will definitely see you again soon," he said, standing up and trying to regain his balance.

The big tits obsession...

"What's your cup size?"

 It was a frequent question from the men who were looking for a woman with large breasts as they could clearly see from my ad pictures that I was a curvy, busty lady.

"I really do not know the size, maybe a D cup," I answered, slightly bored and annoyed with the question.

"Can I come over your big tits?

"Do you do tits wanking?"

These were the types of questions I heard on a daily basis when I advertised as busty lady. The perfect marketing strategy was to often change the title of my ad and ad some new pictures now and then .The funnier it sounded the better as men were often intrigued by such eye catching titles which aroused their curiosity to try something new. I was fully aware that I was not the only escort they went to see and even my very regulars used to go now and then with different girls.

There was always the temptation for men to try something new with somebody else. My pictures were sexy, but not too explicit. Wearing a sexy office outfit with stockings and stiletto heels could be more enticing than being nude, all I needed was to arouse men's curiosity so that if they wanted to see more they had to book. More was less in my case and I liked it. Men always wondered at the size of my breasts and their firmness.

"Are they natural?"

"Wow, they are amazing. You should put some pictures on your ad, it will bring you more clients."

"They are massive, can I lick them?"

"They are proper full breasts, big but not saggy. I love them."

"Can you send me a picture of them? I can have a wank looking at them."

I struggled to understand men's fascination with big breasts, I always wished mine were slightly smaller so that I did not have to wear a bra all the time. I think men have their own fantasies about big breasts and they love to lick and suck them, they love to rub their cock between and they love to see them dangling while they are behind you passionately engaged in a doggy.

"Look at these big tits, "said the young boy, squeezing them together and rubbing his cock between.

He could not have been older than 22, but he seemed quite mature for his age in terms of sexual behaviour. He had a massive cock with a huge and head and had thick veins all along, throbbing with desire.

"Look at my cock baby, look how sexy it is, so big between your huge breasts."

Standing up at the edge of the bed and not being a tall guy he could easily reach my breasts while I was seated on the bed, offering a full view to both of us. His cock felt like a steel pole and looked amazing between the two mounds of white flesh. My breasts started to ache from the pressure of my hands and not wanting him to go on for longer I started to moan, licking my lips and looking straight into his eyes .Few drops of semen hit my cheeks and my lips and I could feel the warmth of it on my breasts and neck. I started to rub it all over my breasts as he squeezed the last drop moaning with pleasure.

"Sorry about that, "he said, extending his had to take a napkin.

"Yes, that was quite a lot," I replied with a crooked smile, pretending to be excited to have his semen all over my breasts. I headed straight to the shower as soon as he left, happy to get rid of the pungent smell of the semen which often made my stomach retch.

The primitive man

Due to the nature of my job I met on a few rare occasions what I call the primitive men. They were purely instinctual and acted as if they were some kind of robot following precisely a set of commands for which they had been programmed to respond. I do not think they were bad men, I think that was the only way they understood sexuality and women. They had no interest in my appearance or idle conversation and they did not bother to stay the whole hour as long as they got what they wanted. I was somehow much happier to finish sooner and as long as they paid my hourly rate I had nothing to object to. They would simply leave their shoes at the door and walk in straight to the couch where they would stand up waiting for me to give them pleasure. They would unzip their pants and would motion me to kneel down, occasionally asking me to take the top off.

"Open your mouth and take it deep, spit on it .I like it sloppy," he asked with a hoarse voice.

His eyes were closed and he seemed to absorb every second of pleasure .Pulling my hair, he started to push his hips, moving his penis fast in and out as if he was fucking my mouth. Somehow my teeth touched his penis and he recoiled wincing in pain.

"That was really unpleasant, you almost ruined my mood .Now you will have to make up for," he said grinning and holding my head still, pulling at my hair.

I could feel the pain at the roots of my hair and the stiffness of my neck, but I was determined to have the job done without complaining. He started to rub his cock all over my face, slapping my eye lids and my lips.

"You like my cock, tell me how much you like it .Show me how much you like it." I wetted my lips and rubbed his penis along them making a steady eye contact.

"You are a little dirty bitch, aren't you? Now open your mouth and take it deep .Suck me again and again, "he said with a devilish grin on his face.

I nodded my head and opened my mouth, taking his cock deep to the root and milking him with my lips as I released it from my mouth.

"You are really good, you do so good baby .I want to come deep in your mouth." I never swallowed and I was terrified by the idea of choking on his semen.

"Could we do on my tongue instead? I think that would be really awesome," I asked winking and licking my lips like a slut.

"Oh you are a real one, a real slut I bet .Open your mouth and stick your tongue out .I'm going to fill you with my spunk."

He came so much that the semen started to drip from the corners of my mouth .I reached for a napkin and spat it out, it was so bitter that I rushed to the toilet and grabbed my strong mint mouthwash from the rack which was above the mirror. I stared at my own image in the mirror and I felt dirty, so dirty that I wished for earth to split and swallow me.

"You really turned into a worthless slut and all for the sake of money, "I thought to myself, overwhelmed with bitterness and disgust. I felt like a living glory hole.

The foot fetish...

"Do you do feet job?" asked the man with a funny accent.

"What do you mean?" I responded slightly puzzled, not knowing what he really meant by that.

"I have a fetish for feet and I would like to see your nails painted in deep red. I want to lick and suck your toes. Can I see you in an hour?"

"Yes, sure I will text you the address. Is there anything else I should know before I do that?" I inquired, wondering what he was really into.

"No worries, I'm a decent guy .I just love feet and red nails "

He was tall and had dark skin and was wearing a pair of black trousers and a light blue shirt. His turban reminded me of Aladdin and the magic lamp .He was very polite and asked me if we could go to the bedroom as he did not like to rush and do things on a couch.

" I'm quite peculiar about the way I like things to go so all you have to do is to comply with requirement .If there is something that you might find unpleasant please tell me."

 His words made me feel safe and I cast away all my previous concerns.

   "Thank you, you are very kind, but I think I'm going to enjoy it," I responded with a big smile.

   "I want you to take your clothes off and lie down on the bed. Would you mind if I draw the blinds aside? I want to look at your naked body in day light."

 Lying on the bed naked in broad day light made feel vulnerable and insecure about my look. I knew that he was going to see my cellulite, my spots and all my imperfections .His eyes were lingering on my body from head to toe and he was silent, seeming to be absorbed with his own thoughts. I started to grow anxious thinking that he might not like what he had just seen. Taking his clothes off, he sat on the edge of the bed and started to caress my feet with his hands.

   "You are very beautiful and you look so natural and fresh, "he said looking into my eyes and smiling.

His words were very reassuring as I have never exposed my naked body to a man in broad day light. I always made sure that I had a subdued light in my flat before I met my clients. He made me feel beautiful and pampered and realized how much a compliment impacts on a person in terms of mood lifting and self confidence. He took my feet in his hands and started to kiss them, nibbling gently at every toe.

   "Do you have some oil? I want to massage your feet."

I always kept a big jar of coconut oil in the bottom drawer of the small white wooden cabinet which was next to my bed. He started to rub the oil on my feet, massaging them as if he were a qualified therapist.

I closed my eyes and my mind wandered back home to my garden. I could almost feel the smell of roses and the smell of the pine trees which enclosed my village. I wanted to freeze that moment forever and never return to reality which was so much the opposite of true happiness. I longed for those days when as a child I lived so freely without the incubus of financial worries, without thinking that one day I will lose my innocence. He stood up and started to undress. The size of his penis woke me up from my reverie.

"Rub my cock and my balls with some coconut oil first. Then put more on your feet and lie down on your back so that you can rub my penis with your lovely small feet."

I knew that this was not going to be an easy job; I knew it would challenge my core strength to some extent. His breath quickened as I started to massage his penis gently, pulling the foreskin back with my feet, rubbing it slowly and then faster, slightly worried that I might cause him some discomfort. His eyes were fixed on my breasts.

"You are giving an amazing foot job. Keep moving faster and faster and play with your nipples, make them hard for me, "he urged me panting.

"An extra task," I thought to myself, struggling to keep my legs up and trying to cope with a sudden pain in my lower back.

I started to rub as fast as I could, hoping that he will finish soon. He seemed to struggle and somehow I got the feeling that this was going to last for some time. I bit my lip as lower back pain increased in intensity, praying that I will keep up with appearances.

"Stop rubbing, "he said, trying to catch his breath.

"I need to kiss you and I have to play with your hard nipples. I was so close to come. I just need a little rest too, no longer in my 30's. And you can have a rest too," he said smiling.

I was relieved, he was kind and sweet. His playful hot tongue worked its magic on my hard nipples, helping me relax and easing the pain in my lower back.

"Are your feet ready to continue our exciting activity? "He asked with a crooked smile.

I put more oil on my feet and started to rub faster and faster determined to make him come in seconds. I felt the warmth of his semen all over my feet and few drops landed on my deep red painted nails. He examined my feet with delight, overly pleased with the result.

"That looks so beautiful. It was an amazing foot job, thank you. I will definitely see you next time," he said, cleaning my feet with baby wipes.

"Pleasure was mutual. Do not worry about my feet too much. I will jump into the shower anyway," I replied with a broad smile.

I was still puzzled as I was struggling to understand why people would have such strange sexual preferences like the foot fetish; to me the feet were just an anatomical part designed to suit the purpose of walking.

The pantyhose ...rape...fantasy

"Do you offer role-play fantasy?" asked the man with a foreign accent.

"Yes, I have several outfits .What is your fantasy?"I asked, hoping that he was not going to be very picky.

"Can you wear shiny pantyhose please? I want a nice role-play for today. I want you to wear a nice white tight short sleeve shirt and a short skirt just above your knees. You mess up with some task and I have to punish you .Do not forget to put a nice pair of stilettos and make up. Make it 5 pm please if you can. Do not wear any panties under the pantyhose and shave down as I like it smooth."

"Yes, sure .We will have a great time. I will text you the address shortly "I answered, trying to conceal my concerns.

 I knew that the task was difficult as it required a great amount of spontaneity and improvisation. Dressed up as required I walked to the entrance door, wondering what he looked like. He was tall and fit, his body was perfect. He looked like a gladiator, muscular and exuding strength and self confidence. He was the kind of man who would not waste too much time with silly things; he knew exactly what he wanted in life.

"You are very, very handsome," I said smiling and trying to control the tremor in my voice.

 I wondered why such a good looking man would pay for sex; he was so handsome that he could have fulfilled his fantasy with a young and beautiful girl without having to pay for it.

"You look exactly like my secretary, I chose you because of the physical resemblance. I always wanted to fuck her hard .Sometimes she can make a real mess about a task and I had to overlook her blunder often. She makes me so angry that I often want to tie her up and fuck all her holes right there in the office "

"You should have fucked her at least once "I retorted, aroused by the entire scenario. I wanted him to be rude and shove me into the wall, I wanted him to penetrate me deeply.

"I think we should go into my study, I have a nice desk there," I said, pointing into the direction of my study.

"Sit down and do not open your mouth until I tell you, "he ordered in a very firm voice.

I sat down, slightly worried and waiting for further instructions.

"You messed up with this project and you deserve condign punishment."

"I'm sorry, I will make sure it does not happen in the future," I answered, trying to look as contrite as I could.

"Stand up and apologise once more," he said, coming towards me.

I stood up and tried to smooth my skirt. His hand slipped between my legs in an instant.

"You are so wet, look at you! You are a horny slut and that's why you cannot focus and you mess up with my work. I'm going to make you beg me to stop," he whispered in a menacing voice.

 My knees felt weak, I was aroused. I wanted him to dominate me and treat me like a whore.

"Turn over and bend over your desk."

I did as requested with the utmost speed.

"God, you have a big ass .You are a real slut with a big ass," he whispered into my ears, his teeth nibbling my earlobe.

He torn my pantyhose and started to knead my bottom so hard that I begged him to stop.

"Turn around and unzip me. Take it in your mouth and feel it. It is all yours bitch, "he said panting.

His cock was of average length, but its girth was considerable. The head of his circumcised penis was so huge that I had to stretch my mouth wide .My cheeks hurt.

"Suck me like a bitch, take me deep, "he said in a guttural voice, pushing my head with his right hand.

He pushed it so deep that my my throat hurt and I started to struggle for air.

"Enough of that stand up! Sit on the desk and spread your legs! " he commanded me, panting with wild excitement.

He slid his cock inside me so abruptly that it made me scream. He took his tie off and rolled it up into a wad. He crammed it into my mouth and started to pound into me mercilessly, making me orgasm so hard that I bit the tie , desperate to release my mouth and breathe.

"Turn around "he said, taking the tie out of my mouth.

He started to lick my cheeks and my ass hole, spreading it as wide as he could.

"I could drink champagne from your ass hole, "he whispered, trying to penetrate me there.

"No, not there please. I never had anal sex," I said, hoping that he would comply.

He stood silently for few seconds and then he plunged deep into my pussy, tearing my shirt and kneading my large breasts with both hands.

"You have such a tight pussy, a slut with a ravenous tight pussy, that's what you are .I'm going to fuck you so hard that you will scream and beg me to stop," he whispered, pulling my hair and slapping my bottom.

"I'm going to fill you up slut, I did not come in a long time, "he said panting and pushing deep into me.

His big balls were slapping my clit, making me come for a second time. I screamed so loudly that he had to put his palm against my mouth to muffle the sounds. He came hard, his cock throbbing inside me, sending waves of pleasure throughout my body.

"You know, I think I'm going to fire my secretary .You would do a better job," he said grinning.

"I would not mind .It was one of the most intense sessions "I replied with a broad smile.

A client with special needs...

A client with special needs is usually the type of client who comes to me when nobody else can do the job. He was short and skinny and his appearance unkempt. His face bore the mark of early teenage acne, it was scarred and blotchy .His dull voice and his tendency to stutter had made me suspicious and wondered if I could have handled such a client as he could have misunderstood the terms of our deal. I always wanted to make things clear on the phone before the client showed at my door. A client with very poor English or one who could not express himself clearly could have made the situation very difficult.

"What exactly do you want me to do?" I asked, not wanting to leave room for any ambiguity.

"Just do what you do with your regulars," he answered in a dull voice.

"I offer massage with happy ending. I also offer full service, but no anal, "I replied in a firm, clear voice.

"Ok, I come for full service. Can you do in 30 minutes?"

I hesitated for a second, wondering if it would be too risky to accept his proposal.

"Yes, you are lucky that I do not have another client soon. I usually do not take bookings at such a short notice.

I was always extremely careful about men who wanted bookings at such a short notice as they could have been loitering about , having nothing else to do and very likely not having the money to pay for even half an hour.

I sized him up from head to toe and reluctantly invited him to follow me to the living room .I noticed that his shoes were very clean, he left them at the door before he followed me. I motioned him to take a seat on the couch, hoping to break the ice with some idle conversation as he seemed to be quite shy.

"I have a girlfriend, but she is away. I like it rough and she does not like it .She said that it is too rough for her," he said with his eyes fixed on the floor.

"What do you mean? You like rough sex?" I asked, worried that he might be into some nasty stuff.

"No, not sex .I do not want sex. I like a very hard hand job and it takes long to come," he answered with his eyes fixed on my breasts.

I knew that I was in trouble and my hands would be really sore after this, but he was there and it was too late for a no. I urged him to take his clothes off and suggested some oral stimulation for the beginning, hoping that it might help. After twenty minutes of licking and sucking hard my cheeks were in terrible pain.

"I guess this is not going to work," I said with a fake smile, not wanting to upset or irritate him.

"Let's try with some sex, "he said grinning. His teeth were yellow and decayed .I thanked God that I did not have to kiss him.

"Just suck me a little bit more to keep me hard," he continued, extending his hand to grab a condom from the small marble table.

I rolled the condom on his penis with my mouth, he did not seem to enjoy it too much.

"Kneel down, I want to fuck you from behind," he said, standing up and positioning himself behind my bottom.

I was not wet and my pussy was so tight that he was almost on the brink of giving up.

"Pass me the lube please," I asked, pointing my index to the small table.

He was finally deep inside me, pushing so hard and rubbing it in and out so fast that I was scared the condom might break.

"Slow down please, you do not want that condom to break," I whispered, trying to conceal my irritation.

He stepped back and discarded the condom into the small pedal bin.

"You see this is my problem. I had this problem with all my ex girlfriends .All of them left me because I like hard like that. I will never come if it is slow," he said, lying down on the bed.

"What about the hand job you mentioned? We can do that," I said hoping that this will work and it will be all over soon.

"Yes, but put plenty of oil. You have to do it fast and tight."

I started to rub his cock with one hand as hard as I could and after 10 min my hand would hurt so badly that I had to stop.

"You stopped, I was so close, "he said, visibly irritated.

"I'm not superwoman sweetheart. I will have to swap one hand for the other, "I answered opening and closing the palm of my hand in an attempt to alleviate the pain.

"I will pay you extra, please make me come. That's why I go to escorts .This time do not stop, I was so close to come."

I starting to rub his cock fast, swapping one hand for the other .He came after 15 minutes of an exhausting hand job. Sweat was dripping over my face and between my breasts and my both hands were aching.

"You did it, you are good. I went to other girls and they could not do it," he said, cleaning himself with the baby wipes.

I was glad it was all over and I knew that there was not going to be a second time. I promised myself not to do this again regardless of the amount of money involved. It was one of the most exhausting sessions I ever had.

The powder man...

Stephen had a good paid job in PR .He used to visit me once a week for his special talcum powder treatment. I could have never imagined myself enjoying a talcum powder experience which sounded a little bit weird, but it proved to be very exciting. I always thought that the baby powder was designed for babies and not for adult play. Stephen was very fond of a fully shaved pussy and he made sure that I was freshly shaved every time he came to see me. He would bring his own shaving kit and would shave my pussy, making it smooth like a baby's bottom. I found the experience very arousing and I think that every woman should try it at least once with her partner. It can be a very intimate and mutually arousing experience and it can simply be part of the foreplay.

"Do you really like to shave women? " I asked him smiling.

"I do enjoy shaving women down there .It makes me so hard when I see the soft puffy lips .They are so soft and silky, I love soft silky things. Sometimes I go into one of these shops where they sell pure silk fabric .I get aroused when I touch the silk, it makes me think of a freshly shaved pussy. I think all women should wear only pure silk outfits, it looks and feels incredibly sexy."

"I could not agree more Stephen. I loved silk underwear and silk clothing though they could be quite expensive, "I said, standing up and looking at my pussy.

"You did a great job, can you pass me the little mirror? I just want to have a look."

It looked lovely and so sexy that I thought all women should do it. I'm sure that most men would agree with me.

He undressed and handed me the talcum powder, lying down on the bed and waiting for me to spread the baby powder over his penis and his testicles. He was fully shaven and the skin was deliciously soft. My hand moved lightly over his balls and cock, spreading the powder all over, making him moan softly.

"That feels amazing .Just rub my balls and penis lightly, very lightly. Take your bra off and come closer."

He took the talcum from my head and spread plenty all over my breasts and pussy. He played with my nipples, tugging and teasing until I begged him to stop.

"You torture me with such unbearable pleasure," I whispered softly, searching his eyes to see his reaction.

"I'm glad that you enjoy it. Lift your leg and put it on the bed so that I can see your pussy. I want to look at it, it feels so sexy and soft," he answered, adjusting his pillow so that he could have a full view of my pussy.

 He rubbed my pussy with the powder which was now having his undivided attention. My right hand kept rubbing gently his penis which felt as hard as steel in my hands.

"Put more powder please, it feels a little dry. Put plenty and rub gently, but fast near the top. Do not go so much to the root of my cock. You can make me cum this way, "he said, handing me the talcum.

His eyes were fixed on my pussy while his deft fingers rubbed gently the puffy lips, caressing and teasing until I could no longer bear the pleasure. I moaned loudly and came so hard that I thought I would faint.

"You are so wet now, wet like a river, "he whispered, delighted to have had such an effect on me.

"I think it is my turn now and I hope I give you as much pleasure as you gave me, "I answered rubbing faster, excited and waiting for the semen to come out in fitful spasms.

 I always took pleasure in seeing a man ejaculating .I enjoyed the power I had over him, knowing that he was entirely at my mercy and a slave to the pleasure.

"Keep doing it. I'm going to come soon," he said, staring at my pussy and rubbing it.

Stephen came a lot as usual. I was amazed with the amount of semen which was dripping through my fingers and to the sides of his tummy.

"Do you have any special diet? I have never seen a man coming so much, "I asked with a broad smile.

"I do not eat anything special or take pills or something. It has always been this way .I guess I could have had many children if I were married, "he answered, laughing.

An ex pilot from Kuwait...

Given the nature of my job I had the chance to meet very interesting and funny people whose first sexual encounters had taken place in funny places or at a very early age. I made a habit of asking my clients about their favourite food and favourite places to visit and most important about their first sexual experience. I think our childhood and our first sexual encounter play a significant role in shaping the character of a person as adult. We are in a way the result of cumulative ongoing sensorial and emotional experiences to which we relate more or less on a daily basis.

Saad was short and overweight and his belly almost protruded from his shirt. He was very well dressed and he seemed to be very pleased with my compliments on his taste for good, quality clothes.

"I always shop on Oxford Street and I have another three gold watches like this one," he said, pointing his index to his wrist watch.

I knew that he had good money and I was very aware that I was not the only one he came to see for entertainment. When people have money they often get bored and they want to try something new most of the time. Saad was no exception and he admitted to it in the most sincere way.

"I have been married two times and have four children. I built houses for both wives, but I knew I was not going to be married for a long time. I liked to have sex many times a day and with different women. Neither of them had ever complained as I like to satisfy them as well," he said, with a broad smile.

"It looks like you are insatiable," I answered smiling.

He had a huge cock and I could have easily imagined why women must have been happy to have had sex with him. He told me clearly that he wanted a good massage and oral and that at his age he was not so much interested in sex.

"He is just lying about it," I thought to myself.

I knew that old or young men think of sex most of the time.

"I was a pilot for 9 years in Kuwait and when I was younger I was a football player. You see this belly was not here before, I injured my knee and my calf and could not play football anymore. I had surgery and now I have terrible pain when I walk. That is why I put so much weight," he said, panting and lying down on my massage table.

"Tell me a little about your life if you like. Have you been sleeping with many women?" I asked in a warm voice, starting to massage his neck.

"I'm sure you could write a book about that sweetie. When I was young I used to have sex with three or four women each day. When I was a pilot I wanted to be naughty with all the stewardesses .I had a nice room in a hotel and as soon as I landed I made arrangements to have ladies coming to my room. Once I had two of them and we had a threesome. We had sex all night long and I came 6 times that night. I will never forget it."

"Six times? You must be joking? I could never imagine that a man would come so many times in one night," I replied, impressed with such an achievement.

"I was very young and very horny .I could have had nonstop sex I think. Please press harder on my lower back as I have terrible pain. Do not forget my ankle and my feet," he asked, not seeming to be bothered with my questions.

"You certainly sound like you had a very interesting life and I want to ask you about your first sexual experience. If you do not want to talk about that is fine. I understand."

"I will tell you everything you want to know. Maybe one day you write a book about me. I was 12 years old when that happened."

"Twelve years old? You had sex when you were 11 years old?" I asked, thinking that he must have been joking.

"You see you interrupted me. Let me tell you the whole story and then you can ask more questions," he answered, slightly irritated with being interrupted.

"I was 12 years old as I told you. My mom sent me to bring a parcel from our neighbour who was living close to us, maybe 10 min walk. She was 40 years old and had 5 kids with whom I used to play. She gave me the parcel and I was about to leave when she looked straight at the zipper of my pants."

"You have something wrong with the zipper, it looks like is broken," she said, coming close to me.

"She unzipped me and took my limp cock out. She knelt down and started to suck me. My cock grew bigger and bigger and the pleasure I felt I will never forget. I came into her mouth and she swallowed it all."

"You were just a child and she was a child abuser," I said in an angry voice.

"No, I liked it. I could have run away if I wanted. I went to play with her kids many times after and she did it to me many times. Since then I had been addicted to pleasure and to women. There is nothing I did not try and I wish I were younger so that I have a lot of pussy."

He left relaxed and happy with my massage. I was still thinking of his story and of his meaty huge cock.

Urethral toys...

George phoned me that morning and asked me if we could try something different this time. He has been one of my very regular clients with whom I exchanged limericks on a weekly basis. He was one of the very few clients with whom I kept in touch after our meetings took place. George was a real gentleman to whom I could confide all the ups and down of my job .He was extremely polite and a good listener and we always had good conversation. He loved the way I played with his cock.

"You look so sexy with my cock in your mouth, "he used to say smiling.

I liked the tone in his voice when he said that to me. He made me feel sexy and attractive. His cock was big, too big for my mouth to accommodate all of it. He never pushed my head to take it deeper, he knew that I was going to do my best. I loved his cock which was extremely responsive to my mouth and tongue, throbbing and almost begging me not to stop.

"Please feel free to tell me about whatever you want to try George. You know that I'm a very open minded person," I told him in a very reassuring voice.

"I know you do not offer any BDSM stuff, but I always wanted to try something new. I hope that you do not mind if I ask you to do this," he said, pausing and waiting for my reply.

"I did some light domination, but nothing rough. What would you like to try?" I asked, very keen to know the answer.

"I bought some very interesting stuff like a nice cock and ball ring plus some urethral toys. I have never tried this with somebody and I want to do it with somebody I feel comfortable with. I hope I did not scare you. I also want you to tie me up, I like the idea of you being in control. That excites me a lot."

Urethral toys were definitely something very new to me, but I wanted to try them. I was slightly worried that it might cause him pain to put something through his penis.

"Bring your stuff and we do it George. I look forward to it. "

"I will bring a bag with all the stuff I have. See you tomorrow at 12.15."

I was excited and slightly scared at the same time; I would not have liked to disappoint George .He emptied his bag on the bed and like a curious kid who had a heap of toys before his eyes, I started to examine them one by one. I set aside the bed restraint kit and the cock rings and asked him which one of the urethral toys is his favourite.

"I like that cock ring, the bigger .Keep that one please. My favourite urethral toy is the the big one, "he said, pointing to what looked like a quite thick plastic tube with stainless steel ends.

"I'm scared that it might hurt you," I said, wondering how such a thing could go through that very tiny hole into the penis.

"Look we try the other one .Just put plenty of lube on it. Do not worry, I tried both of them on and I loved it," he answered, pointing to the ribbed one which was much thinner and made of soft rubber.

He placed the rest of the toys back into the bag and took his clothes off. I fastened his arms and legs to the bed and sucked his balls and his cock which started to grow. I placed the rubber ring on his cock and hid balls with some difficulty which made him wince in pain.

"I hope that did not hurt too much," I said, sucking and teasing his balls which to my surprise looked very sexy and felt lovely to play with.

I sucked his cock and took it deep down my throat, making him moan softly.

"You can squeeze my balls firmly. I will let you know when you should stop," he urged me, slightly panting.

I squeezed his balls and sucked him deep and fast .He started to move his hips as if he wanted to set up the speed with which his penis would go into my mouth. He was fucking my mouth and breathed heavily. My cheeks hurt. I released the monster from my mouth and asked him if we could try the urethral toy. I placed lube liberally on the ribbed toy and slid it inside his penis, looking at the the very tiny beads disappearing inside his penis. I was shocked to see how quickly and smoothly it went inside, making him moan with pleasure.

"This is feeling so nice, put your fingers around my penis. You can feel the beads inside my penis. Twirl the rod between your fingers."

"Yes, I can feel them. It does not hurt you?" I asked, still worried about the pain.

"No, it is very pleasant and it stimulates my prostate. I will have a very intense orgasm. You can take off the ring. Keep playing with my cock, using your mouth and your tongue. The end of the urethral toy felt so nice in my mouth and one or two beads would come out   as I sucked his monster. I took the beads out gently with my lips and then slid them back one by one, torturing George with unbearable pleasure. I sucked him faster and faster and pulled the full length of the toy out, continuing to suck him faster and faster. He filled my mouth with his semen and his body shook for good minutes. He seemed unable to move or talk.

"That was quite something. It must have been a very intense orgasm, I have never seen somebody shaking like this after climax."

"When the end reached my prostate I felt the same way I felt when the semen was at the base of my cock and was about to come. It is hard to explain, but this is different from ejaculating during sex. It is a new and very intense sensation which can easily make a man addicted to it," he said, moving towards the sink to wash the urethral toy.

Water sports and face sitting

"Do you do water sports? "asked the man with an Italian accent.

"Yes, I do piss into a man mouth and sit on his face, but I'm not submissive. I do not like man to piss on me," I explained to him in a firm and clear voice.

I knew what he meant by that. I heard about water sports from one of my escort friends who was a submissive and a receiver. She would go into frenzy when men pissed over her body, but she never allowed a man to piss in her mouth.

"I would never let a man piss in my mouth. I find that really degrading and I think it is the perfect example of the way you objectify a woman. I watched some of the porn videos and they were horrible," she said to me when sat in a coffee shop on a rainy Sunday.

"I think they do it for money, I do not think any woman would really like that. You see most of the stuff women do in porn is the kind of stuff which maybe very few women like in real life. Men watch the crap and they get the wrong idea, they assume that all women like it," I answered, taking another sip.

"You forgot something," she said in a grave tone as if it was a very serious issue.

"You forgot to say that piss tastes horrible," she continued, bursting into laughter.

"How do you know what piss tastes like?" I asked, laughing.

"I know because I tasted mine, I was just curious. I would not let any guy to piss in my mouth even if he would have offered to pay more," she answered wincing with revulsion.

I could not agree more as I disliked even the idea of a man urinating over my body. It was something that I decided not to do from the beginning when I started to work as an escort. I would not debase myself in such a way regardless of how much a man would have offered me. To have a man pissing in my mouth would have made me feel like a public toilet.

"No, thanks," I thought to myself.

I had no problem with abusing a man's face and pissing in his mouth. I found myself quite enjoying it. Rocco was an Italian divorcee in his 40's and was very much into water sports. He loved to lick and suck pussy.

"I could lick and suck pussy all day long .I never gets enough of it," he confessed to me the first time we met.

"I'm sure that most women would like to hear that .You should have been gigolo .Sometimes I laugh when I see men advertising for gigolo and posting a picture of their bulge to show how endowed they are. You do not need a monster cock to please a woman, you just have to perform a good cunnilingus," I replied back with a broad smile.

"I like what I heard! I like what I heard," he repeated to me, shaking his head and making nuzzling sounds as if his nose were stuck between some pussy lips.

Rocco liked to be dominated and he would not want me to wear anything except for a pair of stripper shoes and black sheer stockings. I loved my sessions with him as he was one of the best pussy teaser, he made me come several times, licking the juice with great relish. He would be silent and submissive, waiting for me to fill his mouth with the golden liquid. The secret in order to enhance the pleasure of pissing was to do it little by little so I became a big fan of Kegel exercises which were a fantastic bonus for my pussy ; it made my pussy tight , enhancing my pleasure during intercourse.

I put the leather red collar and the leash around his neck and ordered him to lie down on the floor, on the large PVC sheet. I squatted and straddled him with my thighs, bringing my fully shaved pussy close to his mouth. He stuck his tongue out, searching for my pussy. I pulled his hair and pressed my pussy against his lips and his tongue which flicked my clitoris with great skill. I came hard, crushing his mouth with my pussy which was overflowing with my own juice. I grasped the leash and stood up, asking him to open his mouth wide. I let a little bit of urine to come out, enough to fill out half of his mouth.

He swallowed it down his throat with relish, licking his lips and looking straight into my mouth. I squatted and straddled him again, moving my hips back and forth frantically, crushing his mouth and his face with my pussy. I held his nose between my thumb and my index finger tightly.I moved faster, making myself come so hard that I hardly noticed him bucking beneath me. He was retching and struggling to breathe. I released his nose from my grasp and I stood up, looking him in the eyes. He opened his mouth wide, waiting for me to fill his mouth. I positioned myself at the right angle and peed in a nice forceful stream which he enjoyed tremendously.

He drank it all to the last drop.

The porn star experience

I would not really call it the porn star experience. I would rather call it messing about with a woman in the worst way possible. I did it once in my 5 year career and had sworn to myself to never do it again .It was a very intense, painful and exhausting experience during which I was very close to end up with anal and vaginal tears . It happened when I started to work as an escort, when the only idea about what porn experience looked like was similar to what a porn star experience looked like in the few porn movies I used to watch when I was too horny. I never thought of how those girls felt like, I assumed that they enjoyed since they moaned so loudly, pretending to have an orgasm.

Nacho was half Spanish and half Italian. He phoned me that late afternoon to ask me if he can have a porn star experience. He offered me double the money I charged for my services and tempted by money my answer was an unequivocal yes. I put on one of the sexiest short dresses I had and chose a pair of very high red suede sandals which were matching the dress perfectly. I wondered what Nacho looked like; his voice sounded very mature and firm on the phone. I was always at disadvantage as I had no clue about what my clients looked like while they knew exactly what I looked like from my ad pictures. I rushed to the door with trepidation, hoping that I made the right decision.

He was tall and well built, but not muscular. He did not look like one of those guys who spent hours in the gym and who would have had a lot of stamina. He looked rather like the average guy across the street with whom you would go out for a drink. He handed me the envelope with the money and we walked together to the bedroom.

"Please excuse me for a second .I shall be with you shortly," I said with a broad smile.

I became very careful about the money as several clients managed to steal my money when I made the mistake to put it in a drawer from where it could be easily taken. I secured the money in a vault which was hidden in my wardrobe and went to the bedroom where Nacho was waiting for me naked. He was standing up and to my horror his penis was extremely big, very long and thick and erect. I almost regretted my quick decision, but I knew there was no way out; I had taken the money and it would have been too late to change my mind.

"The show must go on," I thought to myself, sighing.

"I like it nasty .You are my nasty girl today," he said, lifting me in his arms and throwing me on the bed.

"Face on the pillow," he ordered me, unzipping my dress and rolling it over my head.

He removed my bra and my panties and ordered me to kneel down with my face in the pillow. I was terrified at the thought of having that monster up to its root in my pussy. I knew that my womb would scream in pain as it did with other clients who were less endowed than Nacho. He knelt down behind me and licked my ass hole and my pussy and then slapped my bottom so hard that I screamed. He spit on my pussy and inserted his huge cock to the root .I screamed. I begged him to stop.

"Please do not go so deep .We have a womb, please do not forget that. Move as fast as you can, but do not go deep .I want to enjoy it as well," I asked him in a warm voice, not wanting it to sound like an imposition which could have irritated him more.

Nacho did not go deep, but he pounded continuously into my pussy for good 40 minutes in various positions, making my pussy so sore that I begged him for a break. The pain was excruciating after continuous rubbing for good 40 minutes and I was very worried that I could not see any other client for a couple of days. He started to slap hard my face and my breasts with his monster, calling me his nasty bitch.

"I can finish you with my mouth if you want," I said, hoping that he would be happy with that.

"I have not tried your ass baby. Turn around on your knees, I want to fuck your ass from behind and finish there .I want to fuck your ass deep," he replied, slapping my ass hole with his penis.

I was scared that he might hurt my ass so badly that hospitalization might be needed. The only things that had been in my ass before were some dildos of different sizes which I used during intercourse in order to make my vagina tighter. I urged him to pass me the back door lube, hoping that it will make the experience less painful. I screamed hard when he pushed his cock inside and tears were running down my cheeks as he pushed deeper.

"Not to the root please .I'm an anal virgin, believe me or not, "I begged him.

"I love your tight ass nasty babe, "he answered, moving his monster in and out.

He fucked my ass for good 20 minutes which to me had seemed like eternity. The bed sheet was stained with blood; my both holes were so numb that I could not say from which one the blood had come.

About men and women...

I have been working as an escort for almost 5 years and still I could not fully comprehend why men would pay for sex. I made a habit of asking some of my clients to explain to me why a man cannot be loyal to one woman for the rest of his life.

"There are things that a man cannot not do with his wife or his girlfriend. I think he would not dare to ask them to do certain things because he might be scared of being rejected or he simply would not ask because some women are very conservative and not so open minded about sex."

"It is in the DNA. A man needs to spread his seed so he needs to fly like a bee from flower to flower and pollinate."

"Then why do they have to marry?" I asked quite amused with such a puerile explanation.

"Because they need somebody to go to, they need a place to go to in the end of the day," he answered with a smile.

"So you are telling me that men cannot live alone or maybe they are scared of the prospect of being alone for the rest of their lives, "I answered emphatically.

"Yeah, I guess you are right," he retorted, sounding quite bored with the topic.

"What is your favourite food?" another man had asked me.

"Well is hard to say, but I think the answer is sushi. I love sushi."

"So if I give you sushi once a day for 365 days in a row would you not get tired of it?"

"I might not," I answered laughing, knowing what he was intimating to with his remark.

I think most men cheat because they are bored, they would no anything to escape routine and reality .I think men who pay for sex can clearly distinguish between love and sex and they just want sexual satisfaction without the obligations and responsibilities of a long term relationship. Paying a woman to have sex with is mere instant sexual gratification and nothing else. I doubt that these men, maybe except for few, were thinking about me once they returned to the tedium of their daily living. They did not even know my name.

I think there is a disparity in the way men and women relate to sex, love and loyalty. I once watched a very interesting documentary; it was about the story of the two brains. To get to a man's heart a woman needs to get to his penis first while with women things are pretty different: to get where a man wants to put it he needs to get to the woman's heart first. Sex is one of the most powerful instincts and I think men and women are very different in the way they relate to it emotionally. If men might struggle to resist the urges of inserting their penises into different vaginas, women would very likely struggle to understand why men cannot get enough with the woman they have at home.

I think when women cheat they usually do it when they are not sexually and emotionally satisfied with their current relationship or they do it for the sake of being even when they discovered that their man was cheating.

I think both women and men do mistakes; it is easier to pay for sex than to try to rekindle the passion with your partner. They expect a marriage to last forever without putting any effort into constantly fuelling the passion which at some stage was designed to fade, which would be replaced by friendship, caring and compassion. A mutual ceaseless effort is needed to keep the fire burning.

 Be always attentive and complimentary to your partner and do your best to surprise your partner sexually. Always find time for intimacy without suffocating your partner.

It might sound strange to give women advice, but I had seen a lot and I had learned a lot about men during five years. Be honest with your man and tell him what you like and how you like it to be done. Do not be shy with your man .Ask him about his fantasies, try some role-playing and dirty talking. Learn to love and accept your body with all its imperfections. Make sure that you have a wide range of lingerie, sexy costumes and high heels.

 I think every woman can look like a real sex bomb if she puts make up, wears nice lingerie and very, very high heels. I think women do a lot of injustice to themselves when they underestimate their physical charms. Men do not care too much about cellulite believe me.

 "Nobody looks good in the morning, "I said once to myself.

 Look at those girls and women in the glamour magazines, without those expensive clothes and make up they would look pretty average. Fantasy plays a very important part in our sex life; it is the fuel for a long and lasting sexual fulfilment. There are no boundaries in terms of putting your sex fantasies into practice as long as there is mutual consent and enjoyment. If you love your man you have to love his penis .Don't be afraid to please your man with your mouth, he will become your slave. Men are crazy to have a woman going down on them. Why do you think men go to escorts?

"My woman likes to open her legs for me to go down on her, but she never wanted to go down on me. I would not be here if she would have liked it."

"My wife would never play with my ass, I would not even dare to ask her."

Most men go to escorts because they love anal play and a good blow job. If you do not know how to do it then learn, there are plenty of videos about fellatio and anal play. You might discover that you would really enjoy playing with his ass and having him playing with yours. Enjoy pleasing your man orally, he will adore you. He will reward you with an amazing cunnilingus; show him how to do it to you.

Become an expert about pleasuring your man with your mouth regardless of what age you might be. As men age they need more stimulation in order to get erect and your exquisite oral skills might be the perfect way to have him ready for intercourse, or you can simply finish him with your mouth .He will be delighted to see how much you love him.

I oscillate at the moment between continuing and quitting my job as a call girl. I do not think it is financially rewarding anymore and I will probably have to look for an extra part time job. I think in the 70's or 80's it must have been quite a glamorous job when very likely an escort girl would have been taken to a dinner or shopping before the fun happened. Now there is plenty of fish in the pond as thousands of girls offer their services on different websites and often too cheap. Nowadays escorting is more about being a cheap porn actress with whom men want to perform more and enjoy less.

"How many times can a come in one hour?"

Sadly, that was the most common question during my five years of working as a call girl in London.

www.ingramcontent.com/pod-product-compliance
Lightning Source LLC
Chambersburg PA
CBHW051444140726
47987CB00006B/2531